Samuel J. Barrows

The Doom of the Majority of Mankind

Samuel J. Barrows

The Doom of the Majority of Mankind

ISBN/EAN: 9783337387914

Printed in Europe, USA, Canada, Australia, Japan

Cover: Foto ©Andreas Hilbeck / pixelio.de

More available books at **www.hansebooks.com**

THE DOOM

OF THE

MAJORITY OF MANKIND.

BY

SAMUEL J. BARROWS.

BOSTON:
AMERICAN UNITARIAN ASSOCIATION.
1891.

.

.

UNIVERSITY PRESS:

JOHN WILSON AND SON, CAMBRIDGE.

PREFACE.

THE great discussions in theology, both in England and America, during the last few years, have turned mainly upon two points. The first of these is the relation of humanity to the Future Life. In England the discussion on this subject was powerfully stimulated by Canon Farrar's book, "Eternal Hope." In America the debate, rekindled by this book, received a new direction and an independent impulse from the so-called Andover Controversy; one result of which was that an Orthodox clergyman, called to a professorship by the Trustees of that institution, was denied confirmation by the Board of Visitors, because of his charitable speculations on this subject. Candidates for ordination were afterwards excluded from Orthodox pulpits for the same reason. A conspicuous feature in this discussion has related to the destiny of those — involving the great majority of the race — who have no opportunity in this life to accept or even to become acquainted with the Orthodox theory of salvation. With this question before it, the American Board, at its last annual missionary meeting at Portland, refused to concede that the heathen might have a probation after death, and reaffirmed the motive for missionary work to be the necessity of saving them from an endless hell.

The second great subject of theological discussion has been the scientific criticism of the Bible. The influence of Dutch and German criticism has penetrated to the very centre of Calvinistic strongholds.

These two theological questions are much more closely related than they seem to be at first. The Orthodox estimate of the Bible as an infallible book has had much to do in determining what view shall be taken of the future destiny of the race. It was a deep conviction of the close relationship of these two questions which led Rev. George E. Ellis, D.D., of Boston, to affirm in a public address, that before Orthodoxy could revise its creeds, it must revise its estimate of the Bible. In the prolonged discussion which this paper awakened, an incidental statement of Dr. Ellis, that certain Scripture texts " are alleged as certifying that the vast majority of the human race are to be victims of endless woe," was challenged by an Orthodox clergyman, Rev. J. L. Withrow, D.D., of Park Street Church, Boston, who characterized it as an absolute and abominable misrepresentation of Orthodoxy. As editor of the " Christian Register," the writer replied at length in the columns of that paper, aiming to fix upon Orthodoxy the responsibility of teaching this doctrine of the doom of the majority of mankind.

This debate, and the questions that grew out of it, have furnished the material for this book. In the first three chapters the evidence presented in the original article has been largely augmented, especially with reference to modern authorities. In the fourth chapter important admissions and criticisms of Evangelical writers are presented concerning the moral difficulties of this doctrine. Attempted mitigations, and features which are still unrelieved by these palliations, are considered in succeeding chapters; while in a final chapter attention is invited to what seems to us a more promising and, indeed, the only adequate solution.

Two things have become evident in this discussion. First, that Orthodoxy is not wholly ready to revise its belief; and secondly, that its beliefs are constantly suffering revision without its consent. The tenacity, painfully apparent, with which Orthodox bodies hold to ancient standards and traditional interpretations of Scripture, has not prevented the action of other solvents. The old creeds cannot be exposed to the atmosphere of to-day without disintegration. The progress of science, philosophy, and ethics has rendered progress in theology imperative. It has also become evident to an increasing minority of Christians that Orthodoxy must revise its teachings. But no revision will satisfy the demands of an enlightened liberal thought and sentiment, which does not reconsider and restate the relations of God to human destiny, and reaffirm, with clarion voice, the great truth that "in every nation he that feareth God and worketh righteousness is accepted with him," and that "as many as are led by the spirit of God, these are the sons of God."

No apology is needed for any warmth and earnestness in dealing with a dogma so distressing to the feelings, so alien to the moral sense, as the Doom of the Majority of Mankind; but earnestness and warmth are not inconsistent, we trust, with kindly feeling and fairness of statement. In exposing the errors of Orthodoxy, we are not ungrateful for its truths.

No better proof of the timeliness of this volume can be given than that Orthodoxy is earnestly seeking for a solution of the problems of which it treats. That solution may not be reached in the present discussion, but its attainment is only postponed. Fundamental questions in ethics or religion are not decided finally until they are decided rightly. They may be evaded or deferred ; but they will reappear, and knock at the door of the reason and the conscience till by their importunity they command a hearing. The disposition of Evangelical Christians to grapple anew with these old questions is a grateful sign.

There is a liberal spirit working through all the sects to-day. No sect has any monopoly of it, and none can escape its influence. It is not merely pulling down, but it is building " with a sure and ample base," upon broader and deeper foundations. We hail with joy every conquest that it makes. Let the liberal elements in every branch of the Christian Church join hands for the consummation of this constructive work. What are differences in polity, ritual, and denominational traditions, compared with the work of purifying Christianity from its corruptions, developing its best ideals, and making it truly representative of universal religion ?

BOSTON, May, 1883.

CONTENTS.

THE DOOM

MAJORITY OF MANKIND.

———◆———

"Dark and Awful:" such are the words with which an eminent professor in an Evangelical Theological Seminary (Rev. W. G. T. Shedd, D.D., of Union Theological Seminary, New York) describes the doctrine that he teaches to his pupils, and proclaims from the pulpit as the great motive for missionary effort. What is this "dark and awful" doctrine? It is that "millions upon millions"[1] of a "miserable and infatuated race," involving the vast majority of mankind, are doomed to everlasting woe.

Were this merely the personal opinion of the man who teaches it, we should hardly think it necessary to consider it, notwithstanding the respect we entertain for this eminent writer and scholar. If it were the opinion of a few individuals only, or if it were a doctrine antiquated and obsolete, we should not arraign it in this paper. But it is a view which has been and is still extensively held within the limits of what is known as Evangelical Christianity. It is a doctrine upon which a whole system of theology has been built, and upon which it still rests.

[1] The Guilt of the Pagan, New York, 1864, p. 23.

Three hundred years ago John Calvin, in describing his doctrine, used words similar to those of Dr. Shedd: "It is a dreadful decree, I confess." *Decretum quidem horrible, fateor.* And yet this dreadful decree has been, and still is, proclaimed as a part of the glad tidings which Jesus Christ brought into the world!

At the present day there are many who, while admitting the premises upon which the doctrine is founded, shrink from the conclusions to which it inevitably leads. They would gladly relieve Orthodoxy from the charge of having believed and taught that "the vast majority of the human race are to be the victims of endless woe." They cannot feel more deeply than we do the reproach of such a doctrine. We welcome any argument or any confession which shall remove this stigma from the name of Christianity. But such argument or confession must be true to the facts. Orthodoxy cannot be relieved from its responsibility for this doctrine by the plea that it has never authoritatively taught it.

Rev. J. L. Withrow, D.D., pastor of Park Street Church, Boston, is amazed that men should so "absolutely and abominably misrepresent the Evangelical belief concerning the number of the saved and lost."[1] When a prominent Orthodox minister feels called upon to deny that he personally believes that the vast majority of the human race are to be victims of endless woe, we are conscious of increased respect for his opinions and his courage in declaring them; but when it is flatly denied that it is a doctrine of the system of Orthodoxy which he represents, the negation demands consideration.

In the following pages we respectfully present some competent evidence upon the subject, — not so much that we may fix the shame and disgrace of the doctrine upon Evangelical Christians, as that we may have some ground for urging them to remove it. The best argument we can

[1] Christian Register, December 14, 1882; and January 4, 1883.

present against this dismal doctrine is to let those who hold it state it for themselves. The evidence we offer covers the following points: —

I. Evangelical Christians have taught this as a Scripture doctrine.

II. It is taught by Evangelical Creeds.

III. It is still taught by Evangelical Denominations.

We purpose to take these points in the order in which they are given, and consider them in detail.

I.

THE DAMNATION OF THE MAJORITY OF MANKIND HAS BEEN TAUGHT BY EVANGELICAL CHRISTIANS AS A DOCTRINE OF THE SCRIPTURES.

When it is asked, "Do the Scriptures teach this doctrine?" we answer, With any fair, reasonable, scholarly interpretation, they do not. But we do assert, without fear of successful contradiction, that *Orthodoxy has infused its interpretation into the Scriptures, and has constantly appealed to them in support of this doctrine.* The texts which are adduced in its support are very numerous, and the men who have presented them have been as numerous as the texts. They have not been confined to any one age. In his book, "Mercy and Judgment," which followed the storm created by "Eternal Hope," Canon Farrar has gone into this general question in much detail. As a result of his examination he says: "I assert and shall prove that the *Christian writings of every age abound in assertions that the few only will be saved.*" Canon Farrar proves his assertion by referring to the opinions of the Church Fathers. Rev. F. N. Oxenham, in his book, "What is the Truth as to Everlasting Punishment?" also in reply to Dr. Pusey, has effectually appealed to the same sources. Some of these quotations

show from what a small tincture of Scripture, diluted
with a great deal of individual speculation, the doctrine
was compounded. They are sufficient to confirm Mr.
Oxenham in his conclusion that "the dominant teaching
of all sorts of theologians since the Reformation, both
Catholic and Protestant (with no doubt a remarkable
exception here and there), until the last few years, has
declared unhesitatingly this doctrine as a certain and
terrible truth revealed to us by God." (p. 31.) ,

ST. CHRYSOSTOM.

St. Chrysostom, in his Twenty-fourth Homily on the
Acts, preaching at Antioch, said: —

" How many, think you, are there in our city who will be
saved ? It is a terrible truth which I am about to utter, but
yet I will utter it. Among so many thousands, a hundred cannot be found who will be saved, and even about them I doubt."
(*Opp.* ed. Montfaucon, ix. 198 [214], B.)

ST. AUGUSTINE.

" Not all, *nor even a majority, are saved.*" (*Enchiridion*, cap.
24, al. 97. *Opp.* vi. 231 [395], ed. Bened.)

" They [the saved] are indeed many, if regarded by themselves, *but they are few in comparison with the far larger number* of
those who shall be punished with the devil." (*Contra Cresco-
nium*, lib. IV. cap. 63, al. 53. *Opp.* ix. 514 [785], ed. Bened.)

GREGORY THE GREAT.

" Many come to (the knowledge of) the faith, but *few are led
on to enter the heavenly kingdom.*" (*In Evang. Hom.* xix. c. 5.
Opp. i. 1513, ed. Bened.)

ST. THOMAS AQUINAS.

St. Thomas Aquinas, commenting on 2 Pet. i. 10, says: —

" For now it is a secret who are elect and who are reprobates, since both are now together ; and many, who now are

living well, are nevertheless reprobates, and many, who now
are evil-livers, are nevertheless elect. But in the Day of Judgment, when God will winnow and purge his floor, it will then
be evident who are elect and who are reprobates ; *and that the
elect are few and the reprobates many, since much shall be found
of chaff and little of wheat.*" (See Oxenham, p. 150.)

CORNELIUS À LAPIDE.

Writing on the "great multitude which no man could
number" (Rev. vii. 9), Cornelius à Lapide, the eminent
commentator, says : —

"From what has been said, we may estimate that in the end
of the world the total number of all the saints and elect, who
have ever lived anywhere in any age, will make up some hundred
millions. The number of the reprobate will, however, be far
greater, which will come to not only hundreds but even thousands of millions. For often out of a thousand men, — nay, even
out of ten thousand, — scarcely one is saved."

Cornelius says elsewhere that " a crowd of men sink
daily to Tartarus as thick as the falling snowflakes."
(Num. xiv. 30.)

GIULIO CESARE RECUPITO.

Recupito was the author of a curious book, "De Num-
ero Prædestinatorum et Reproborum," Paris, 1664. We
have never had access to it; but Canon Farrar found a
copy in the Archbishops' Library at Lambeth, and thus
describes it : —

" In the first chapter he argues that the number of the elect
is fixed and definite. In the second he quotes the view of those
who held that the number of the lost did not exceed that of the
saved. He does not stop to argue the question generally. He
at once assumes, as an axiom, that for six thousand years none
but Jews could have been saved, and that now none could be
possibly saved outside the pale of the Church; so that countless
millions of Mohammedans, Gentiles, and heretics are calmly
disposed of with the oracular remark that 'their damnation is
certain.'

" He next adduces the opinion of the Fathers, and quotes in his favor St. Chrysostom, St. Ambrose, St. Augustine, and St. Gregory. Then he tells us from the Abbot Nilus, a revelation to St. Simeon Stylites that scarcely one soul was saved out of ten thousand, and the vision of a bishop, referred to by Trithemius in his ' Chronicon,' about A.D. 1160, in which a hermit appeared to him, and said that at the hour of his death three thousand others had died, and that the only one saved among them was St. Bernard of Clairvaux, and three who went to purgatory. He further adduces another vision of a preacher who says that sixty thousand stood with him before God's bar, and all except three were condemned to hell ; and yet another of a Parisian master who appeared to his bishop, announcing that he had been damned, and added that ' so many souls were daily thrust down to hell that he could scarcely believe there were so many men in the world.' Indeed, he asked if the world still existed. For he had seen so many tumbling into the abyss that he thought that none could remain alive."

DU-MOULIN'S SCRIPTURE PROOFS.

Dr. Lewis Du-Moulin was Professor of History at Oxford. We have before us his little work, found in Harvard College Library, and bearing the following title : —

" Moral Reflections upon the Number of the Elect, Proving plainly from Scripture Evidence, etc., That not One in a Hundred Thousand (nay probably not One in a Million), from *Adam* down to our Times, shall be Saved. By Dr. Lewis Du-Moulin, Late History Professor of Oxford. London : Printed for *Richard Janeway*, in *Queens-Head* Alley, in Pater-Noster-Row, MDCLXXX."

The doctrine of this book may be inferred from the title ; but we quote some interesting passages : —

" Some, who are but few in Number, as *Cælius Secundus Curio, de amplitudine regni gratiæ*, have indeavoured to prove, That the Number of the Saved Ones, is much more great, than that of the Damned. Others make almost an equal division of them, as *Zuinglius:* But the *most* believe, that the Number of the Damned is incomparably greater, than those that are / Saved; and that there is not above one Saved of a hundred Thousand, or rather of a Million, from *Adam*, even to the Day of Judgment." (p. 1.)

"*Jesus Christ* sayes, that his Flock is small ; that there are but few persons that enter into the Kingdom of Heaven ; that when he shall come again upon the Earth, he shall not find faith in it ; that all the World shall run after the Beast: That the Number of the Elect is very little in Comparison of those that are Called, and Consequently, that the Number of the Called is infinitely less, than that of those who are not Called, and that know not what the *Christian* Religion is. For if you suppose that before *Jesus Christ* there was but one Called among a Hundred Thousand, if not indeed a Million of Men, and that among a Hundred *Called*, it was but a peradventure that one was Chosen ; the Number of the Elect before the Advent of *Jesus Christ* will amount to very little ; for it is easy to shew by History, that, I will not say of a Hundred, but of Five Hundred, or a Thousand Called in *Israel*, scarce will you find one Faithful ; insomuch, that though the Called People were so greatly numerous, the Prophets, particularly *Esaiah*, complain, that hardly one believed their Report, or Preaching." (p. 11.)

" To conclude, I would refer my self to the judgment of any sober, considering person, what a vast and almost an infinit proportion in number one should find, if from *Adam's* days down to ours, there should be a comparison made of the Sum total of the Elect, with that of those who are not Elected : I believe that this Proportion would be of one Person Saved, to a Million that is not : that is to say, That there is a Million of Reprobates to one that shall be Chosen so as to be Saved." (p. 21.)

But there is another authority. Let us take the man who, more than any other, has been adduced as the champion and founder of the Orthodox system, — John Calvin. His modern influence we believe is certainly declining, but he is still proudly appealed to as an authority by a great body of Evangelical Christians. Professor E. D. Morris, of Lane Seminary (Presbyterian), in his Inaugural Address recently delivered, says : " Presbyterianism throughout the world may be said to be in an eminent sense doctrinal, — doctrinal because it is Calvinistic." What is, then, the doctrine of Calvin on this point?

CALVIN'S SCRIPTURE PROOFS.

Calvin believed, and did not hesitate to assert, that the majority of mankind are eternally lost. He did not fear to face the logical consequences of his belief. Where did he get his belief from? He professed to get it — and certainly thought in all honesty that he got it, from the Bible. He claimed that the Bible taught that God had elected a *few* to eternal glory, but that the rest, including the heathen, who constitute the vast majority of mankind, were reprobated to eternal damnation.

In his commentary on Matt. vii. 13, Calvin says : —

" He expressly says that *many* run along the *broad road*, because men ruin each other by wicked examples. For whence does it arise that each of them knowingly and wilfully rushes headlong, but because, while they are ruined in the midst of a *vast crowd*, they do not believe that they are ruined. The *small number of believers*, on the other hand, renders many persons careless. It is with difficulty that we are brought to renounce the world, and to regulate ourselves and our life by the manners of a *few*. We think it strange that we should be forcibly separated from the *vast majority*, as if we were not a part of the human race. But though the doctrine of Christ confines and hems us in, reduces our life to a *narrow road*, separates us from the crowd, and unites us to a *few* companions, yet this harshness ought not to prevent us from striving to obtain life." (*Pringle's Translation.*)

In his Harmony, Matt. xxiv. 22, he discusses the question why God determined that " a *few* should remain out of *a vast multitude*."

In his comments on Matt. xxiv. 5 he shows that it was " through the vengeance of God that *more were carried away by a foolish credulity* than were brought by a right faith to obey God."

In commenting upon the prayer of Jesus, in John xvii. 9, he says : —

" Whence it appears that the whole world does not belong to its Creator ; only that grace snatches *a few* from the curse and wrath of God, and from eternal death, who would otherwise perish ; but leaves the world in the ruin to which it has been ordained."

In remarking upon the beautiful words of Christ, *Come unto me, all ye that are weary and heavy-laden,* Calvin's dreadful views are clearly made plain : —

" And yet all [who accept this invitation] are *few in number;* because, out of the *innumerable multitude* of those who are perishing, but few perceive that they are perishing."

In writing against Arminianism Calvin confesses this horrible doctrine to its full extent : —

" I ask again, how has it come to pass that the fall of Adam has involved *so many nations with their infant children* in eternal death, and this without remedy, but because such was the will of God? Here the tongues that have been so voluble it becomes to be mute. It is a *dreadful decree,* I confess." — (*Institut.* lib. iii. 23, 7.)

OPINIONS OF OTHER COMMENTATORS.

As Jesus was journeying towards Jerusalem, teaching in cities and villages, Luke tells us (xiii. 23) that a certain man met him and said unto him, " Lord, are there few that be saved ? " It was a curious question, but one very natural for a Jew to ask; for it was a common belief among the Jews that they were the elect of God, and that the Gentiles were of little importance in his sight. Eisenmenger[1] quotes a rabbin who said that " the soul of a single Israelite is by itself more precious and dear in the sight of the blessed God than all the souls of a whole nation;" and again: " The world was created for the sake of the Israelites." " They are the wheat, the other nations

[1] *Entdecktes Judenthum,* vol. i. pp. 569, 571.

are the chaff." It may have seemed to this Jew a dangerous doctrine to preach that the Gentiles were equally
the children of his favor ; as centuries later it seemed to
the makers of the Westminster Catechism a "detestable
and pernicious" doctrine that the heathen could be saved.
But whatever the motive of this question, Jesus did not
deign to answer it.   He advised his questioner, however,
to *strive* to enter the strait gate himself, to *work out* his
own salvation, instead of cherishing the idea that he
belonged to a favored class.

Although Jesus did not satisfy this man's curiosity by
giving his own views on the subject, it seems a little
strange that there should have been commentators in all
ages who have been bold enough to furnish him with an
opinion.   With singular frequency the conclusion has
been reached that few were to be saved and the vast
majority eternally lost.   Among Calvinistic commentators this has been the unanimous verdict.   That system
of orthodoxy has permitted no other belief.   But this
view has not been confined to Calvinists.   It has been
held by Arminians as well.   As Canon Farrar[1] says :
"It is centuries older than Calvinism; it is immensely
wider than the limits of Calvinistic churches."   And
again in the same book : "The damnation of the vast
majority of mankind has been the normal teaching of
theologians in every age since the earliest."   (p. 140.)

The passage in Luke has furnished less ground, perhaps,
for this conclusion than two that occur in Matthew —
namely, Matt. xx. 16 and xxii. 14, where Jesus says,
"Many are called but few chosen."   In one case it follows
the parable of the Laborers, which seems to be directed
against the doctrine of Jewish exclusiveness; in the other
it follows the parable of the Marriage of the King's Son.
In neither parable is there the slightest reference to
the doctrine of everlasting punishment.   Jesus was re-

---

[1] Mercy and Judgment, p. 153.

buking the people of his own age and country because many of them preferred darkness rather than light. He showed also that, though many were called into his kingdom, but few became eminent in it. It is a monstrous assumption to suppose that in these passages he gave a revelation concerning the proportion of the human race who should be consigned to hell. Yet this is the view that has been taken over and over again of these texts by Evangelical writers. Matt. vii. 13 has been interpreted in the same way. A few extracts from prominent commentators will show how persistently these texts have been interpreted with reference to the final destiny of the race.

DIODATI.

Diodati, in his Annotations (third edition, 1651) on Matt. vii. 13, says: —

" For to come to eternall happiness doe not follow the way of pleasures, and ease of the world and the flesh, nor *the great number and multitude of men:* but make choice of the hard and laborious profession of the Gospel with its crosse : and joyn thyself to the small sanctified flock of the Church by faith and imitation of good men, *who are alwaies the smallest number in the world.*"

On Matt. xxii. 14 he says : —

" Because that many who are called do not answer to Gods call and that even amongst those also who doe in some sort answer, some are rejected, it appears that the *eternall election is not of all, but of a few.*"

On Luke xiii. 23 he says : —

" Christ according to his wonted custome does not answer directly to that curious and unprofitable question: *but silently avoweth that indeed there are but few.*"

ESTIUS.

Estius, commenting on St. Paul's declaration (1 Tim. ii. 4) that " God will have all men to be saved and to come to the knowledge of the truth," concludes one part of his argument by saying, " Since *it is certain* that all men are not saved, and that all men do not believe, *but only a few out of all*," &c.

And, again, on 2 Pet. iii. 9, he says : " Since, then, *it is an admitted fact* [constet] that all men do not come to repentance, but that *the majority are lost*, it is inquired," &c.

WESTMINSTER ASSEMBLY OF DIVINES.

In the Annotations made upon the Bible by the Westminster Assembly of Divines, they say of Matt. xx. 16 : —

" Some come short of that which others, inferior to them in the account of the world, obtain, because they are only outwardly called, by the word, but are not from eternity chosen by God to eternall life. . . . Though there are many who are externally called, yet there are but few that go to heaven."

On the similar passage in Matt. xxii. 14, they say : —

" Because many that are called do not come into God's Church, and among those that do come, some are not saved, for want of an holy conversation, it appears that *few are chosen to eternal life*."

MATTHEW HENRY.

Matthew Henry, on Matt. vii. 13, says : —

" Those that are going to heaven are but few compared to *those that are going to hell ;* a remnant, a little flock like the grape-gleanings of the vintage; as the eight that were saved in the ark."

In commenting on the question put to Jesus in Luke xiii. 23 : " Are there few that be saved ? " Matthew Henry recognizes the fact that Jesus did not return any direct answer to the question. He does not, however, seem content to leave the matter where Jesus left it, but proceeds to answer the question himself.

" We have reason to wonder that, of the many to whom the word of salvation is sent, there are so few to whom it is indeed a saving word. . . . It concerns us all seriously to improve the great truth of the fewness of those that are saved. Think how many take some pains for salvation, and yet perish because they do not take enough; and you will say that there *are few that will be saved*, and that it highly concerns us to strive. . . . Think of the distinguishing day that is coming, and the decisions of that day, and you will say there *are few that shall be saved*, and that we are concerned to strive. Think how many that were very confident they should be saved will be rejected in the day of trial, and their confidence will deceive them ; and you will say, there *are few that shall be saved*, and we are all concerned to strive."

WILLIAM BURKITT.

William Burkitt (vicar of Dedham, Eng., 1712), on Matt. xxii. 14, says : —

" Amongst the Multitude of those that are called by the Gospel unto Holiness and Obedience, few, *very few comparatively*, do obey that Call, and shall be Eternally saved."

ADAM CLARKE.

Dr. Adam Clarke, in his commentary on Psalms ix. 17 : —

" The wicked shall be turned into hell, and all the nations that forget God. There are both *nations* and *individuals* who, though they *know* God, *forget* Him, that is, are *unmindful* of Him ; do not *acknowledge* Him in their designs, ways, and works. These are all to be *thrust down into hell*."

In his commentary on Matt. vii. 14 he says (Italics his) : —

" There are *few* who *find* the way to heaven ; fewer yet who *abide* any time in it ; fewer still who *walk* in it ; and fewest of all who *persevere* unto the end."

The " wide gate and broad way " he interprets as leading into " eternal misery."

On Matt. xxii. 14 he remarks : —

" Many are called by the preaching of the gospel unto the outward communion of the Church of Christ ; but *few, compara-*

tively, are chosen to dwell with God in glory, because they do not come to the master of the feast for a marriage-garment."

DODDRIDGE.

Doddridge on Matt. vii. 14 : —

" Strait is the Gate and rugged and painful the Way which leads to eternal Life, and they who find it and with a holy Ardency and Resolution press into it, so as to arrive at that blessed End, *are comparatively few.*"

On Matt. xx. 16 : —

" Though *many are called,* and the Messages of Salvation are sent to vast Multitudes, even to all the Thousands of Israel, yet there are *but few chosen.* A *small remnant* only will embrace the Gospel so universally offered and so be saved according to the Election of Grace, while the rest will be justly disowned by God as a Punishment for so obstinate and so envious a Temper."

On Matt. xxii. 14 : —

" Though it be a dreadful truth, yet I must say that even the greatest part of those to whom the Gospel is offered will either openly reject or secretly disobey it. . . . *Few are* chosen in such a sense as finally to partake of its blessings."

BOOTHROYD.

Boothroyd's Family Bible (1824), in a note on Matt. xxii. 14 : —

" Though many are invited [by the Gospel] yet few chosen, — few that *will be finally approved.*"

HEUBNER.

Heubner, on Matt. vii. 13 : —

" Oh, how many go on the broad way! Thus the *majority of men* hasten to ruin, and will ultimately be condemned."

DR. OWEN.

Dr. John J. Owen, in his commentary (New York, 1857) on Matt. xxii. 14 : —

" Many are invited to the blessings and privileges of the gospel feast, but comparatively few are real participants of the grace of God. This was true of the Jewish nation, in respect to whom this parable had primary application. The people in general were obdurâte and unbelieving, while a few only listened to the inspired prophets. Such, also, is the sad *fact in respect to every nation*, even those most highly favored with the light of pure Christianity. The *masses go down in impenitence to the grave*, and *comparatively few are found in the way that leadeth to life.*"

BISHOP OF LINCOLN.

Dr. Christopher Wordsworth, Bishop of Lincoln (1872), on Matt. xxii. 14 : —

" Christ commands to *baptize all Nations*. . . . He proffers the Marriage garment to all, and yet how many refuse it and prefer their own clothes! Besides, even of those who have the wedding garment, some are described as *bad*. Therefore *few are chosen*. The κλητοὶ, or *Ecclesia visibilis*, is numerous, but *how few are the chosen !* "

OLSHAUSEN.

Olshausen, on Luke xiii. 23, 24, concedes the damnation of the majority : —

" The Saviour in reply does not say exactly that there were but few who should partake of salvation, for, looked at simply in itself, the number of the saved is great; it is only *relatively, and as compared with the lost*, that *it is small.*"

DEAN GOULBURN.

Speaking of the doctrine of the comparative fewness of the saved, Dean Goulburn, in an *excursus* added to the second edition of his sermons on Everlasting Punishment (1881), says : —

" It is awfully startling, and ought to be very rousing to the energies of our will, to think how legibly this doctrine is written on the surface of Holy Scripture, — what pains, if I may say so, God has taken to impress it upon us for our warning." (p. 241.)

2

" Now let it be observed that this doctrine of the fewness of
the saved, in comparison of the lost, is one so plainly revealed
that none who accept Holy Scripture as the word of God, can
dispute it." (p. 251.)

We have quoted from a line of commentators extending from Calvin down to the present day, to show how
constantly this doctrine has been attributed to the Scriptures. There have not been lacking eminent scholars who
have formed a more rational judgment of these passages,
but the view we have given has been the more common
one, and has helped to confirm the popular belief on this
subject.

OTHER AUTHORITIES.

This interpretation of the Scripture is frequently confessed in the works of prominent Evangelical writers.

Richard Baxter, in his " Saints' Rest," thus describes
the people of God : —

" They are a *small part of lost mankind* whom God hath from
eternity predestinated to this Rest for the glory of his mercy,
and given to his Son, to be by him in a special manner redeemed." (*Baxter's Saints' Rest*, ch. viii. 115.)

Flavel, in his " Method of Grace," says (the italics are
his) : —

" *How great a number of persons are in the state of condemnation!*
That is a sad complaint of the prophet, — ' Who hath believed
our report? and to whom is the arm of the Lord revealed ? '
(Isaiah liii. 1.) Many talk of faith, and many profess it; but
there are few in the world unto whom the arm of the Lord has
been revealed in the work of faith with power. It is put among
the great mysteries that Christ is believed on in the world
(1 Tim. iii. 16). Oh, what a terrible day will be the day of
Christ's coming to judgment, when so many millions of unbelievers shall be brought to his tribunal to be solemnly sentenced."

Rev. Jonathan Townsend, M.A., pastor of a church at
Needham, said : —

" And thus quick are we all hastening into Eternity. Some to heaven, a *little Company;* but *Multitudes* throng the way to Hell, a *great Multitude which no Man can number.* " (*Discourse on God's Marvellous Sparing Mercy,* 1738, Boston. p. 5.)

It is competent to quote President Edwards on this point : —

" That there are generally but few good men in the world, even among them that have those most distinguishing and glorious advantages for it, which they are favored with that live under the Gospel, is evident by that saying of our Lord, from time to time in his mouth, *Many are called, but few are chosen.* And if there are but few among these, how few, how very few indeed, must persons of this character be, compared with the whole world of mankind! The exceeding smallness of the number of true saints, compared with the whole world, appears by the representations often made of them as distinguished from the world." — (*Edwards on Original Sin,* section vii. ; *Works,* vol. ii. p. 343.)

Another form in which the doctrine is taught is, that the great body of the heathen world — numerically the vast majority of the race — are doomed to eternal misery. In " The Principles of the Protestant Religion, maintained by the Ministers of the Gospel in Boston," 1690, by James Allen, Joshua Moody, Samuel Willard, and Cotton Mather, the damnation of the heathen is taught as a Scripture doctrine : —

" That there are any Elect among Pagans, who never had the gospel offered them, is not only without Scripture warrant, but against its Testimony, as hath been agen and agen made evident." (pp. 92, 93.)

In a work entitled " The Doleful State of the Damned," by S. Moody of York, Maine, published in 1710, we find the tortures of the heathen thus described : —

" The Gentile Nations that perished (by Thousands and Millions) for lack of Vision, for so many Ages, whiles God (in a way of New Covenant Mercy) knew only the Jewish Nation, the Seed of Abraham; giving His Word to Jacob, His Statutes and Judgments to Israel: All these Nations (I say) whom God suffered to walk in their own wayes, will be inraged with Self-tormenting Madness, that the Lord should send all His Servants the Prophets to them, unto Jacob whom He loved, and make His Word in their Mouth, effectual to the Conversion and Salvation of so many Thousands of them; while these Sinners of the Gentiles could not hear for want of a Preacher, Rom. x. 14. And the Ungospellized Nations, now since Christ. came and brake down the Partition Wall between Jews and Gentiles (which are by far the greatest Part of the World), will have the same bitter Pill to Chew, while they Consider how that some in all Ages, of one Nation or other, and some of all Nations, in one Age or other, are Redeemed and Saved; this will make them Lament and Blaspheme, that the Gospel was not sent to their Nation, and in their Day on Earth. Now to take the whole World of Reprobates together, in whatever Age or Nation they lived, that Perish either for lack of Vision, or for Rebelling against the Light of Nature and Scripture both; we may a little consider, in a more general Way, how it will Vex and Torment all the Damned, while they View and Survey in their Heaven-piercing Thoughts, the Place and State of the Glorified; and consider, 1. That there was a Possibility of their having been all happy, as well as they that are so, or instead of them; there being nothing in the Nature of God or Man against it; . . . so that Thousands of Millions will say, in Hell (and vex themselves forever with such fruitless Wishes) Oh! That the Gospel of Salvation had been sent to us: Oh! That we had but heard the joyful Sound: Oh! That we had Lived in such Times and Places as were blessed with Sabbaths, Ministers, and Bibles. And ten thousand Times ten Thousand, Oh! That the Gospel had been made effectual to us." (*The Doleful State of the Damned*, Doctrine II. p. 47.)

Rev. Nathanael Emmons, D.D., was one of the most eminent of Orthodox theologians. His name needs only to be mentioned to be recognized and honored as one of Orthodoxy's representative champions. His writings have had a wide circulation and influence. The writer possesses an edition of the Works of Dr. Emmons, with an interesting Memoir by Prof. Edwards A. Park. It is not the work of a Latin Father; it bears the imprint of the Congregational Board of Publication, 1860. In the second volume of that work, Dr. Emmons has a sermon entitled "Sins without Law deserve Punishment," in which he gives Scripture evidence to show that the heathen (constituting the vast majority of mankind) shall finally perish : —

"The design of this discourse is to show : —

I. That the heathen are without law.

II. That they sin without law. And

III. That they must perish without law." (vol. ii. p. 663.)

"Though the heathen sin without law, yet their sin deserves eternal destruction." (*Ib.* p. 668.)

"Though God has never forbidden the heathen to do things worthy of death, yet since they have done things worthy of death, he has a right to make them suffer eternal death, the proper wages of sin." (*Ib.* p. 669.)

"God has told us *in his word*, that the heathen, who sin without law, shall perish without law. God might, if he had pleased, have saved the heathen, notwithstanding their desert of eternal destruction; but he has let us know in his word that he determines to cast them off forever. He has already caused many of them to perish.

"The men of Sodom and Gomorrah were heathen, and them, we are told, he has 'set forth for an example, suffering the vengeance of eternal fire.' David says: 'The wicked shall be turned into hell, and all the nations that forget God.' And he prays for the destruction of the heathen: 'Thou, therefore, O Lord God of hosts, the God of Israel, awake to visit all the heathen.' And again he prays: 'Pour out thy wrath upon the heathen that have not known thee, and upon the kingdoms that have not called upon thy name.'

"*More passages* might be quoted, and more things said upon this head, but it is needless to enlarge. The will of God respecting the state of the heathen seems to be *clearly and fully revealed in his word.*" (*Ib.* p. 669.)

Rev. Enoch Pond will be recognized as another eminent Orthodox authority. In a course of Missionary Discourses,

given at Ward, Mass., and published in 1824, we find one
on Romans vi. 21: "The end of those things is death,"
in which he says : —

   " We have, therefore, in the text this affecting truth : *the end
of heathenism is eternal death.*   Or, in other words, *the great body
of those who live and die heathen must finally perish.*"   (p. 221.)

   " Like all unpardoned sinners, they are ' condemned already,'
and are under sentence of eternal punishment.   This sentence
cannot be remitted without repentance and reformation.   We
find no intimations in the *Scriptures* that God will forgive any,
even heathens, without repentance ; but everywhere the plainest
intimations to the contrary."   (p. 225.)

   " The conclusion, therefore, is irresistible, that the great body
of the heathen are not delivered from the wages of sin, but are
descending, in fearful multitudes, down to the chambers of
eternal death."   (p. 228.)

   " It is submitted, my brethren, after what has been said,
whether the proposition, announced at the commencement of
this discourse, has not been immovably established, — that *the
end of heathenism is eternal death ; or that the great body of those
who live and die heathens must ' go away into everlasting punishment.*' "   (p. 232.)

   Dr. Pond adduces " numerous passages of Scripture in
which the heathen are represented as exposed to perish
forever."   The list is too long to republish.

   These quotations from acknowledged Orthodox authorities might be easily multiplied ; but we have given enough
to show how Orthodoxy has interpreted the Bible on these
points, and how badly that collection of books has fared
at its hands.   What better argument than such beliefs as
these can we present that Orthodoxy needs to revise its
estimate of the Bible?   What better evidence to show
that the Scriptures had better be rationally interpreted,
or rationally abandoned ?

   Undoubtedly the Scriptures do teach, in the various
texts that have been quoted, that comparatively few attain
the higher blessedness, — the more abundant life, to which

Jesus called men, — compared with the great multitude
who take a broader and easier road. But the assumption
is unwarranted that these passages refer to everlasting
punishment.

DR. EZRA ABBOT'S VIEW.

In a note on one of the most frequently quoted of
these passages, that of Matt. xxii. 14, "Many are called
but few chosen," Prof. Ezra Abbot, of the Cambridge
Divinity School, after quoting, as an instance of intelligent Orthodox interpretation, Prof. Bernhard Weiss's
exposition of this passage,[1] says : —

"I would only add that, in this parable and elsewhere, Jesus
is not considering the question of 'probation after death,' —
whether those who depart from this life without having become
his followers, or even in a state of hostility to his religion, may
or may not, in the ages to come, be brought into a better
spiritual condition; still less is he teaching any doctrine about
election and reprobation in the Calvinistic sense, and the number of the *finally* saved. The present parable describes his
rejection by the great body of the Jews; and also teaches that
of those (Jews or Gentiles) who might profess to be his followers
many would not be truly such, and therefore could not share the
blessings which belonged to his kingdom. When persecution
should test the faith of his disciples, many would fall away;
nay, 'the love of *the* many,' of the great majority, 'would
become cold' (Matt. xxiv. 10, 12). Many would seek to enter
the kingdom, or to partake of the great Messianic banquet, but
would not be able (Luke xiii. 24), from non-fulfilment of the
essential conditions, which were very different from what they
were conceived to be by the great body of the Jews.

"In Matt. vii. 13, 14, Jesus teaches that the path that leads
to life is strait and narrow; *i.e.*, that true religion requires great
self-denial and self-sacrifice, such as the vast majority of men

[1] Weiss, *Das Matthäusevangelium und seine Lucas-Parallelen erklärt*
(" The Gospel of Matthew and its Parallels in Luke Explained "),
Halle, 1875, p. 472. Compare his " Biblical Theology," § 30, *d*, vol. i.
p. 137, English translation.

shrink from, so that those who walk in this narrow path are comparatively few. Everybody knows that this was the state of the Jewish and the heathen world when Jesus uttered these words, and that it is to a very large extent the state of the world now. The questions whether, or how, or when, those who are in the road to destruction can turn round and change their course, are not here considered. To assume that Christ's language teaches that the spiritual state in which a man leaves this world is irreversible, and that the great majority of men, or all men, may not *ultimately* become his followers, is to thrust into the passage what is not there.

" The prevalent false view of this and many other passages is due in part to that misinterpretation of the language of Jesus which* applies such terms as *life, eternal life, salvation, the kingdom of heaven*, etc., on the one hand, and *death, destruction, hell, damnation* (or *condemnation*), on the other, mainly to the rewards and punishments of another world, and conceives of these as more or less arbitrary, and not, essentially, the natural and necessary results of the observance or violation of spiritual laws. It is not recognized that these terms in their essential meaning, as used by Jesus, describe not external conditions, but states of the soul; that ' he who listens to the word of Jesus and believes in Him that sent him *hath* eternal life; and cometh not into condemnation, but hath passed out of death into life.' The pictorial, dramatic, parabolic language in which Jesus enforces the fact of retribution, and illustrates the conditions of admission into his kingdom, is taken in a gross sense, utterly foreign from the spirit of his religion." (*Christian Register*, Boston, Feb. 22, 1883.)

But whatever view may be taken of the Scripture teachings on this point, humanity is rapidly reaching a point of development when it will refuse to receive as authoritative any doctrine which affronts the affections, outrages the moral sense, and blasphemes the name of the Most High.

II.

THE DAMNATION OF THE MAJORITY TAUGHT BY EVANGELICAL CREEDS.

IT is claimed by some that the only fair way in an examination of this kind is not to take individual interpretations of Scripture, or individual utterances on the point at issue, but to appeal to the Evangelical Creeds. Thus Rev. Dr. Withrow, of Boston, in the discussion which has given rise to this book, said: "Evangelical creeds are the constitutional beliefs of Christendom. These great standards of Orthodox belief contain the body of Evangelical Faith, founded on the Word of God. It would be in order for any one to adduce from the Westminster Confession of Faith, from the Thirty-nine Articles, or the Saybrook or the Andover Creed, a disproof of my statement, that 'no evangelical creed in Christendom teaches that the vast majority of the human race are to be the victims of endless woe.' . . . Orthodoxy does not hold itself responsible for all the views of its several adherents. *Its beliefs are to be judged by its standards.*" (*Christian Register*, Jan. 4, 1883, p. 5.)

The position assumed by Dr. Withrow is perfectly logical. It is consistent and honorable. Denominations that have standards to which they appeal should be judged by them. Let us see, then, what the great evangelical standards teach concerning this doctrine. We will not pause here to ask the question how far individuals who still profess these creeds have secretly or openly repudiated them. We are told that we must not judge evangelical bodies by individual opinions. The appeal has been made to the standards; to the standards let us go.

We readily grant that the oldest creed known to Christendom, the Apostles' Creed, does not contain the doctrine; but it is unmistakably taught in the mediæval creeds of the Church, and most conspicuously in the creeds of that branch of the Christian Church to which Dr. Withrow belongs, — Calvinistic Orthodoxy. As our argument concerns only the Protestant belief on this subject, we omit reference to the Roman Catholic creeds, and, beginning with the Protestant Reformation, confine ourselves to those creeds which are still the authoritative standards of a large portion of the Evangelical Church. We do not say that the doctrine of the doom of the majority is stated in so many words, but we contend that a creed is responsible, not merely for its definitions, but for the inevitable conclusions which must be drawn from them. We shall show, therefore, that the principal creeds teach :

1. The doctrine of the eternal damnation of the majority of infants of the race.

2. The doctrine of the eternal damnation of the great body of the heathen world, constituting the vast majority of the adult portion of mankind.

1. Infant Damnation in the Creeds.

1. *The doctrine of the damnation of the majority of infants is taught in creeds which make salvation dependent on baptism.*

This was the doctrine of Augustine. It is the doctrine of the Roman Catholic Church to-day. It is also taught in

THE AUGSBURG CONFESSION.

That Confession, adopted in 1530, says : —

" ART. IX. Of Baptism they teach that *it is necessary to salvation.* . . . They condemn the Anabaptists, who allow not the baptism of children, and *affirm that children are saved without baptism.*"

Luther, in an Exposition of Psalm xxix., in extending
comfort to Christian mothers, based on the invitation of
Jesus, says : —

"We say that children are conceived and born in sin, and
cannot be saved without Christ, to whom we bring them in
baptism . . . for without Christ is there no salvation. Therefore Turkish and Jewish children are not saved, since they are
not brought to Christ."

Melanchthon, who wrote the Augsburg Confession, also
held the same views : —

"The promise of grace pertains to children who are within the
Church. It is certain that out of the Church, — that is, among
those upon whom the name of God is not invoked through
baptism, and who are without the Gospel, — there is no remission
of sins and participation in eternal life." (*Melanchthonis Oper.*,
part. 1. *de baptism. infantum*, fol. 237 *seq.*)

He classes them with blasphemous Jews, Mahometans,
and the enemies of Christ.

Again he says : —

"It is not to be asserted that salvation pertains to infants
outside of the Church, as without any evidence the Anabaptists
furiously contend."

And again : —

"This hypothesis is to be held, that infants who are within
the Church, upon whom the name of Christ has been invoked,
are received into grace; not Turks nor Jews."

Zerneke,[1] the author of a curious book on the " State
of Infants of Heathen Parents, who die in Infancy," after
quoting these passages from Melanchthon, says : —

[1] *Dissertatio Theologica de Statu Infantium a Gentilibus progenitorum,*
cum in Infantia decedunt. Jena, 1733. Third edition, — in the library
of Dr. Ezra Abbot, Cambridge, Mass. We find on the titlepage the
names of Dr. Joannes Fecht as *præses*, and Jacobus Henricus Zerneke
as *respondent ;* but it appears from p. 96 that Zerneke is the substantial
author, though he was assisted by Fecht, Professor of Theology and
Superintendent at Rostock.

" From these it is easily apparent in what way the words of the Apology of the Augsburg Confession are to be understood, since any one is the best interpreter of his own words."

The Augsburg Confession has always been, and still is, the authoritative standard of the Lutheran Church. In the discussion on "The Revision of Creeds" in the *North American Review* for February, 1883, Rev. Dr. G. F. Krotel, speaking for the Lutheran Church in America, says: "All parts of the Lutheran Church in this country profess to receive the fundamental creed of Lutheranism, the Augsburg Confession *ex animo*." He tells us that "the Lutheran Church, instead of going away from her standards, is really coming back to them."

Rev. Dr. C. P. Krauth, the most prominent advocate of Lutheranism in this country, in his principal work, "The Conservative Reformation," argues that Baptism "as the ordinary channel of Regeneration, places infant salvation on the securest ground." In his "Review of Dr. Hodge's Systematic Theology," p. 22, Dr. Krauth relieves us somewhat by saying: "As Lutherans we have a clear faith resting on a specific covenant in the case of a baptized child, and a well-grounded hope resting on an all-embracing mercy in the case of an unbaptized child." But this is the individual view of Dr. Krauth; it is not the teaching of the Lutheran Standards; nor, as we have seen, was it the view of Luther and Melanchthon, the authors of that Confession. There is abundant evidence that Lutheran ministers and laity still cling to the necessity of water-baptism for infant salvation, and, like Roman Catholics, would not dare to let their children die without it.[1]

Dr. Philip Schaff, of Union Theological Seminary in New York, says: —

[1] See a little book, "Behind the Scenes," by F. M. Jams, Cincinnati, Ohio, — G. W. Lasher, 1883, — in which confessions are given of various ministers who have baptized infants to assure parents of their salvation. (Chaps. II. and IX.)

"All Orthodox systems which hold to the necessity of water-baptism for salvation, lead to the horrible conclusion that all unbaptized infants dying in infancy, as well as all the heathen, — that is, by far the greatest part of the human race, past and present, — are lost forever." (*The Harmony of the Reformed Confessions*, p. 50.)

The Church of England, in her baptismal formula, clearly teaches the doctrine of baptismal regeneration; but though maintaining that baptized infants are saved, she does not say that unbaptized infants are lost.

2. *The doctrine of the damnation of infants taught in Calvinistic Creeds.*

In his review of Dr. Hodge's "Systematic Theology," that eminent Lutheran scholar and divine, Dr. C. P. Krauth, lately deceased, has presented an overwhelming amount of testimony concerning "Infant Baptism and Infant Salvation in the Calvinistic System." Calvinistic Creeds and Calvinistic Fathers have been placed on the witness-stand. We have not space to give a tithe of the evidence so thoroughly presented; but, after reading it, we cannot escape his conclusion, that "Calvin's theory involves *the certain damnation of the majority of the infants of the race*, and does not claim that there is distinct evidence, even in the most hopeful case, that any particular child is saved." (p. 58.)

Dr. Philip Schaff, himself a Presbyterian, makes this candid admission: —

"The scholastic Calvinists of the seventeenth century mounted the Alpine heights of eternal decrees with intrepid courage, and revelled in the reverential contemplation of the sovereign majesty of God, which seemed to require the *damnation of the great mass of sinners, including untold millions of heathen and infants*, for the manifestation of his terrible justice. Inside the circle of the elect all was bright and delightful in the sunshine of infinite mercy, but outside all was darker than midnight." (*The Harmony of the Reformed Confessions*, p. 47.)

THE SYNOD OF DORT.

At the Synod of Dort, 1619–1622, this question of infant damnation came up. The position of Calvinism is unmistakable, that only *elect* infants are saved. Against this view the Arminians protested; and their "Apology" shows the doctrine against which Episcopius and others remonstrated : —

" Why shall it be thought absurd or wicked to say that God not only wills of his good pleasure to destroy, but also to devote to the inner torments of hell, the *larger part of the human race,* many myriads of infants torn from their mothers' breasts? for these are the horrid inferences which the school of Calvin rears on those foundations, which consequently the Remonstrants look upon with their whole soul full of aversion and abhorrence." (*Krauth*, p. 63.)

The Arminians say again : —

" We especially desire to know from this venerable Synod, whether it acknowledges as its own doctrine, and the doctrine of the Church, particularly what is asserted . . . concerning the creation of *the larger part of mankind for destruction,* the reprobation of infants, even though born of believing parents." (*Acta Synod.*, 121; *Krauth,* p. 58.)

The Swiss Theologians at Dort say : —

" That there is an *election and reprobation of infants* no less than of adults, we cannot deny in the face of God who loves and *hates unborn children.*" (*Acta Synod.* Judic. 40. See *Krauth,* p. 15.)

From the Zurich Consensus between Calvin and the Zurich ministers : —

" We zealously teach that God does not promiscuously exercise IIis power on all who receive the Sacraments, but only on the elect. He enlightens unto faith none but those whom IIe has *foreordained unto life.*" (*Niemeyer, Collect. Conf.* 195.)

From the above it is evident that, according to Calvinism, non-elect infants cannot be saved by baptism.

Molinæus, 1568–1658, " one of the greatest divines of the French Calvinistic Church," defended the decrees of the Synod of Dort : —

" If one were to crush an ant with his foot, no one could charge him with injustice, — though the ant never offended him, though he did not give life to the ant, though the ant belonged to another and no restitution could be made. . . . The offspring of the pious and faithful are born with the infection of original sin. . . . As the eggs of the asp are deservedly crushed, and serpents just born are deservedly killed, though they have not yet poisoned any one with their bite, so infants are justly obnoxious to penalties." (*Krauth*, p. 66.)

Again, Molinæus says : —

" We dare not promise salvation to any [infant] remaining outside Christ's covenant." (*Krauth*, p. 18.)

The Bremen Theologians at Dort say : —

" Believers' infants *alone*, who die before they reach the age in which they can receive instruction, do we suppose to be loved of God, and saved of His . . . good pleasure." (*Acta Synod.*, 63.)

Marckius (quoted by Krauth) says : —

" Nor is it to be doubted that among these reprobated are to be referred the *infants of unbelievers*. . . . God has revealed nothing as decreed or to be done for their salvation, and they are destitute of the ordinary means of grace. So that we ought *utterly to reject, not only their salvation*, of which Pelagians dream, but also the Remonstrant [Arminian] theory *that their penalty is one of privation, without sensation*. The terminus to which these are predestined is *eternal death*, destruction, *damnation.*" (*Krauth*, p. 35.)

THE WESTMINSTER CONFESSION.

The Westminster Confession and Catechisms, says Dr. Philip Schaff, in his " Harmony of the Reformed Confessions " (p. 11), " present the ablest, the clearest. and the fullest statement of the Calvinistic system of doctrine. . . . They have been adopted not only by Presbyterians, but also, with some modifications, on church polity and the doctrine of baptism, and with a reservation of greater freedom, by the Orthodox Congregationalists and the Regular, or Calvinistic Baptists in Great Britain and America."

This Confession of Faith also assumes the damnation of unelect infants.

"*Elect* Infants dying in infancy are regenerated and saved by Christ, through the Spirit who worketh when and where and how he pleaseth. So also are all other *elect* persons who are incapable of being outwardly called by the ministry of the word.

"Others *not elected*, although they may be called by the ministry of the word and may have some common operations of the Spirit, yet they never truly come to Christ, and therefore cannot be saved." (*Westminster Confession*, Chap. X. iii., iv.)

The inevitable conclusion from this language is that while *elect* infants are saved, *unelect* infants are certainly lost. Modern Calvinists, repudiating the doctrine of infant damnation, would like to put a new meaning into these words; they would have us believe that *all* dying in infancy are elect. But such is not the language, and such is not the natural meaning, of the Westminster Confession. If the writers of it believed that all infants were saved, why did they limit the word *infants* by that word *elect?* In that Confession we are told again that "*every* sin, both *original* and actual, . . . doth in its own nature bring guilt upon the sinner, whereby he is bound over to the wrath of God and curse of the law, and so made subject to death, with *all* miseries, spiritual, temporal, and *eternal.*" (*Westminster Confession*, VI. vi.)

Thus original sin is exposed to the same penalty as actual sin, and nothing in the Westminster Confession relieves any infants but *elect* ones from this fate. There is not a line in that Confession that teaches that infants are saved as a class. As Dr. Krauth says, their salvation depends upon "an absolute personal election."

This view of the Westminster Confession is confirmed by a vast array of testimony from the Calvinistic writers of the time, which we could readily present, if it seemed necessary; but perhaps one quotation will be sufficient to show how the Westminster Confession was understood by the men that made it. Dr. William Twisse was the Pro-locutor of the Westminster Assembly of divines. He was one of the most prominent Calvinists of his day. In his greatest work, "The Vindication of the Grace, Power, and Providence of God," he says : —

"*Many* infants depart from this life in original sin, and con-sequently are condemned to eternal death on account of original sin alone: therefore, from the sole transgression of Adam, con-demnation to eternal death has *followed upon many infants.*" (*Vindiciæ*, i. 48.)

This view of Twisse was very extensively held among Calvinists, not only in England, but in this country. We have a rough poetic monument of its prevalence in this country in " The Day of Doom," by Rev. Michael Wig-glesworth, A. M., "teacher of the Church at Malden, in New England, 1662." This is " a poetical description of the great and last Judgment." Among the great number of those who appear before the judgment-seat are the reprobate infants, who piteously plead for mercy : —

" Then to the Bar all they drew near
   Who died in infancy,
   And never had or good or bad
   effected pers'nally;
   But from the womb unto the tomb
   were straightway carrièd,
   (Or at the least ere they transgress'd)
   Who thus began to plead:

" ' If for our own transgressi-on
   or disobedience,
   We here did stand at thy left hand,
   just were the Recompense;

3

But Adam's guilt our souls hath spilt,
  his fault is charg'd upon us;
And that alone hath overthrown
  and utterly undone us.

' Not we, but he ate of the Tree,
  whose fruit was interdicted;
Yet on us all of his sad Fall
  the punishment 's inflicted.
How could we sin that had not been,
  or how is his sin our,
Without consent, which to prevent
  we never had the pow'r?

' ' O great Creator why was our Nature
  depravèd and forlorn?
Why so defil'd, and made so vil'd,
  whilst we were yet unborn?
If it be just, and needs we must
  transgressors reckon'd be,
Thy Mercy, Lord, to us afford,
  which sinners hath set free.

' ' Behold we see Adam set free,
  and sav'd from his trespass,
Whose sinful Fall hath split [spilt?] us all,
  and brought us to this pass.
Canst thou deny us once to try,
  or Grace to us to tender,
When he finds grace before thy face,
  who was the chief offender?'

" Then answerèd the Judge most dread:
  ' God doth such doom forbid,
That men should die eternally
  for what they never did.
But what you call old Adam's Fall,
  and only his Trespass,
You call amiss to call it his;
  both his and yours it was.

"' He was design'd of all Mankind
    to be a public Head;
A common Root, whence all should shoot,
    and stood in all their stead.
He stood and fell, did ill or well,
    not for himself alone,
But for you all, who now his Fall
    and trespass would disown.

"' If he had stood, then all his brood
    had been establishèd
In God's true love never to move,
    nor once awry to tread;
Then all his Race my Father's Grace
    should have enjoy'd for ever,
And wicked Sprites by subtile sleights
    could them have harmèd never.

"' Would you have griev'd to have receiv'd
    through Adam so much good ;
As had been your for evermore,
    if he at first had stood ?
Would you have said, " We ne'er obey'd
    nor did thy laws regard ;
It ill befits with benefits,
    us, Lord, to so reward ?"

"' Since then to share in his welfare,
    you could have been content,
You may with reason share in his treason,
    and in the punishment.
Hence you were born in state forlorn,
    with Natures so depravèd;
Death was your due because that you
    had thus yourselves behavèd.

"' You think " If we had been as he
    whom God did so betrust,
We to our cost would ne'er have lost
    all for a paltry lust."

Had you been made in Adam's stead,
   you would like things have wrought,
And so into the self-same woe,
   yourselves and yours have brought.

" ' I may deny you once to try,
   or Grace to you to tender,
Though he finds Grace before my face
   who was the chief offender;
Else should my Grace cease to be Grace,
   for it would not be free,
If to release whom I should please
   I have no liberty.

" ' If upon one what's due to none
   I frankly shall bestow,
And on the rest shall not think best
   compassion's skirt to throw,
Whom injure I? will you envy
   and grudge at others' weal?
Or me accuse, who do refuse
   yourselves to help and heal?

" ' Am I alone of what's my own,
   no Master or no Lord?
And if I am, how can you claim
   what I to some afford?
Will you demand Grace at my hand,
   and challenge what is mine?
Will you teach me whom to set free,
   and thus my Grace confine?

" ' You sinners are, and such a share
   as sinners, may expect;
Such you shall have, for I do save
   none but mine own Elect.
Yet to compare your sin with their
   who liv'd a longer time,
I do confess yours is much less,
   though every sin's a crime.

" ' A crime it is, therefore in bliss
you may not hope to dwell;
*But unto you I shall allow
the easiest room in Hell.*' "

Wigglesworth's views were thus in entire harmony with
the Westminster Confession and with those of Twisse, its
prolocutor, Calvin, and others whom we have quoted.
The popularity of his poem was very great. " The first
edition," says John Ward Dean,[1] " consisting of eighteen
hundred copies, was sold, with some profit to the author,
within a year ; " which, considering the population and
wealth of New England at that time, shows almost as
remarkable a popularity as that of " Uncle Tom's Cabin."
   Professor Tyler, in his " History of American Literature," says :[2] " This great poem, which, with entire uncon-
sciousness, attributes to the Divine Being a character the
most execrable and loathsome to be met with, perhaps, in
any literature, Christian or Pagan, had for a hundred
years a popularity far exceeding that of any other work,
in prose or verse, produced in America before the Revolution. . . . No narrative of our intellectual history during the colonial days can justly fail to record the enormous
influence of this terrible poem during all those times.
Not only was it largely circulated in the form of a book,
but it was hawked about the country in broadsides as a
popular ballad. . . . Its pages were assigned in course to
little children to be learned by heart along with the catechism ; as late as the present century, there were in New
England many aged persons who were able to repeat the
whole poem ; for more than a hundred years after its first
publication it was, beyond question, the one supreme poem
of Puritan New England."

[1] New England Historical and Genealogical Register, for April,
1863.
[2] History of American Literature, vol. ii. p. 34.

"His work," says Francis Jenks,[1] "fairly represents the prevailing theology of New England at the time it was written, and which Mather thought might 'perhaps find our children till the Day itself arrives.'" Happily that day has not arrived, and the children of Mather have disowned so much of the doctrine as relates to the damnation of infants.

The Cumberland Presbyterian Church of the United States, which was organized in 1810, adopted in 1813 a semi-Arminian revision of the Westminster Confession. Instead of saying, "Elect infants dying in infancy are regenerated and saved," they changed the language to *all* infants. The great body of the Presbyterian Church in America, however, though they have individually given up the belief in infant damnation, still allow this frightful doctrine to disfigure their standards. Yet Dr. Withrow tells us that Orthodoxy must be judged "by its standards." No modern Presbyterian clergyman that we know of teaches the doctrine of infant damnation, but *every* Presbyterian minister is obliged to subscribe to a Confession which teaches it. If our Calvinistic brethren deny the doctrine of infant damnation, let them blot it out of their standards. *Either their standards are condemned by their present belief, or their present belief is condemned by their standards.*

2. The Damnation of Heathen in the Creeds.

Not only is the damnation of unelect infants and unbaptized infants taught in the creeds, but the damnation of the unconverted heathen, the vast majority of the adult portion of mankind, is taught with even more emphasis and uniformity.

THE SAXON VISITATION ARTICLES.

In the Saxon Articles of Visitation, prepared by the Lutherans in 1592 against the Calvinists, the Calvinists

[1] Christian Examiner, November, 1828.

were charged with holding, among others, the following errors : —

" That God *created the greater part of mankind for eternal damnation*, and wills not that the greater part should be converted and live." (ART. iv. *On Predestination*, 2.)

The Calvinists denied that they taught that God *created* the greater part of mankind *for* eternal damnation, but did not deny that such was their destiny, nor did the Lutherans, generally.

THE THIRTY-NINE ARTICLES.

In the Thirty-Nine Articles of the Church of England, both in the English Edition of 1571 and the American Revision of 1801, we find salvation thus conditioned : —

"ART. XVIII. They also are to be accursed that presume to say that every man shall be saved by the Law or Sect which he professeth, so that he be diligent to frame his life according to that Law and the light of Nature. For Holy Scripture doth set out unto us only the Name of Jesus Christ, whereby men must be saved."

This article is liberally interpreted by the Church of England to-day, although it undoubtedly had its origin in the same narrow view of salvation which is apparent in the extracts from the creeds that follow. Bishop Burnet, in his celebrated Exposition of the Articles, 1699, struggles with the difficulties and mysteries of this article as it concerns the heathen, and shows a charity of heart and breadth of mind which might be commended to many in our own day : —

" As for them whom God has left in Darkness, they are certainly out of the Covenant, out of those Promises and Declarations that are made in it. So that they have no Federal Right to be saved, neither can we affirm that they shall be saved : But on the other hand, they are not under those positive denunciations, because they were never made to them : Therefore since God has not declared that they shall be damned, no more ought we to take upon us to damn them.

" Instead of stretching the Severity of Justice by an Inference, we may rather venture to stretch the Mercy of God, since that is the Attribute which of all others is the most Magnificently spoken of in the Scriptures: So that we ought to think of it in the largest and most comprehensive manner. But indeed the most proper way is, for us to stop where the Revelation of God stops: And not to be wise beyond what is written ; but to leave the secrets of God as Mysteries, too far above us to Examine, or to sound their depth." (*Exposition of the Thirty-Nine Articles.* 4th ed., p. 169.)

THE SCOTCH CONFESSION OF FAITH.

The Scotch Confession of Faith adopted in 1560 is very explicit in excluding the heathen : —

" We utterly abhorre the blasphemie of them that affirme, that men *quhilk live according to equitie and justice sal be saved, quhat Religioun that ever they have professed.* For as without *Christ Jesus* there is nouther life nor salvation ; so sal there nane be participant hereof, bot sik as the Father hes given unto his Sonne Christ Jesus, and they that in time cum unto him, avowe his doctrine, and beleeve into him, we comprehend the children with the faithfull parentes." (ART. XVI.)

THE IRISH ARTICLES OF RELIGION (1615).

" ART. XXXI. They are to be condemned that presume to say that every man shall be saved by the law or sect which he professeth, so that he be diligent to frame his life according to that law and the light of nature. For holy Scripture doth set out unto us only the name of Jesus Christ whereby men must be saved.

" ART. XXXII. None can come unto Christ unless it be given unto him, and unless the Father draw him. And all men are not so drawn by the Father that they may come unto the Son. Neither is there such a sufficient measure of grace vouchsafed unto every man, whereby he is enabled to come unto everlasting life."

THE LAMBETH ARTICLES.

This limitation in the Irish Articles was a reiteration of the same doctrine seen in the Lambeth Articles, a

Calvinistic appendix to the Thirty-Nine Articles, composed in 1595: —

" I. God from eternity hath predestinated certain men unto life ; certain men he hath reprobated."

" III. There is predetermined a certain number of the predestinate which can neither be augmented nor diminished.

" IV. Those who are not predestinated to salvation shall be necessarily damned for their sins."

" VII. Saving grace is not given, is not granted, is not communicated to all men, by which they may be saved if they will.

" VIII. No man can come unto Christ unless it shall be given unto him, and unless the Father shall draw him; and all men are not drawn by the Father, that they may come to the Son.

" IX. It is not in the will or power of every one to be saved."

THE CANONS OF DORT.

The Canons of the Synod of Dort were adopted in 1618 and 1619. They are very strong in their definitions of election, and in their denial of salvation through the light of nature. These Canons are still in force in the Reformed (Dutch) Church in America, and the text from which we quote is taken from the " Constitution of the Reformed Church in America," published in New York (Schaff, *Creeds*, &c., vol. iii. p. 581) : —

" *First head of Doctrine*, ART. VII. Election is the unchangeable purpose of God, whereby, before the foundation of the world, he hath, out of mere grace, according to the sovereign good pleasure of his own will, chosen, from the *whole human race*, which had fallen through their own fault from their primitive state of rectitude into sin and destruction, *a certain number of persons* to redemption in Christ."

" ART. X. . . . He was pleased, out of the *common mass of sinners*, to adopt *some certain persons* as a peculiar people to himself. . . . "

Under the third and fourth heads of doctrine it effectually excludes the heathen : —

" Art. iv. There remain, however, in man since the fall, the glimmerings of natural light, whereby he retains some knowledge of God, of natural things, and of the difference between good and evil, and discovers some regard for virtue, good order in society, and for maintaining an orderly external deportment. But so far is this light of nature from being sufficient to bring him to a saving knowledge of God and to true conversion, that he is incapable of using it aright, even in things natural and civil. Nay, farther, this light, such as it is, man in various ways renders wholly polluted, and holds it [back] in unrighteousness, by which he becomes inexcusable before God."

THE WESTMINSTER CONFESSION.

But we have been especially challenged to quote the Westminster Confession in proof of the doctrine of the doom of the majority, — and strangely enough, by one who has signed the creed, and who professes to accept it. We have already quoted that confession to show that, historically interpreted, it teaches infant damnation. Its belief in the damnation of the heathen is positive, and unambiguous.

" Others, *not elected*, although they may be called by the ministry of the Word, and may have some common operations of the Spirit; yet they never truly come unto Christ, and therefore *cannot be saved:* much less can men, *not* professing the Christian religion, be saved in any other way whatsoever, be they never so diligent to frame their lives *according to the light of nature* and the *law of that religion they do profess;* and to assert and maintain that they may is *very pernicious and to be detested.*" (*Confession*, X. iv.)

In the Westminster Assembly's "Larger Catechism," question 60, the heathen are again condemned : —

" *Q.* 60. Can they who have never heard the gospel, and so know not Jesus Christ, nor believe in him, be saved by their living according to the light of nature?

"*A.* They who, having never heard the gospel, know not Jesus Christ, and believe not in him, cannot be saved, be they never so diligent to frame their lives according to the light of nature or the law of that religion which they profess; neither is there salvation in any other, but in Christ alone, who is the Saviour only of his body, the Church."

We are further told that—

" All that hear the Gospel and live in the visible Church are not saved; but only they who are true members of the Church invisible. . . . The invisible Church is the whole number of the elect." (Q. 61, 64.)

The Westminster Confession and Catechism thus teach: (1) that only elect infants are saved; (2) that only a part of the visible Church is saved; (3) that the heathen who never heard the gospel are damned. It requires no arithmetic to deduce from the Westminster Catechism the doctrine of the " vast majority of the lost." On the contrary, it requires some new and miraculous system of arithmetic to deduce from it anything else.

The older and regular Congregational creeds agree substantially with the Westminster Confession on doctrinal points.

THE SAVOY DECLARATION.

The Savoy Declaration was adopted by the Elders and Messengers of the English Congregational Churches in 1658. It is simply the Westminster Creed corrected to suit the Congregational polity, and excludes the heathen from salvation:—

" This promise of Christ, and salvation by him, is revealed only in and by the Word of God; neither do the works of creation or providence, with the light of nature, make discovery of Christ, or of grace by him, so much as in a general or obscure way; much less that men, destitute of the revelation of him by the promise or gospel, should be enabled thereby to attain saving faith or repentance." (Chap. XX. II.)

The Savoy Declaration adds some words to the tenth chapter of the Westminster Confession, which bolt the door against the heathen more effectually than ever:—

" Others not elected, although they may be called by the ministry of the Word, and may have some common operations of the Spirit, *yet not being effectually drawn by the Father*, they *neither do nor can come unto Christ*, and therefore cannot be saved : much less can men, not professing the Christian religion be saved in any other way whatsoever, be they never so diligent to frame their lives according to the light of nature and the law of that religion they do profess; and to assert and maintain that they may is very pernicious and to be detested."

AMERICAN CONGREGATIONAL CREEDS.

The "Elders and Messengers of the churches assembled in the Synod at Cambridge, in New England," in June, 1648, declare the Westminster Confession, published the previous year, " to be very holy, orthodox, and judicious in all matters of faith ; and do therefore freely and fully consent thereunto for the substance thereof." Finding the Confession doctrinally sufficient, the Cambridge Synod confined itself to an exposition of the Congregational polity.

The Synod of New England Congregational Churches, held at Boston in 1680, accepted and republished the Savoy revision of the Westminster Confession ; passages from which, excluding the heathen from salvation, we have quoted above.

The Saybrook Platform, adopted by the Elders and Messengers of the churches in the Colony of Connecticut, assembled at Saybrook, September 9, 1708, recognizes and endorses the Westminster, Boston, and Savoy confessions as its doctrinal foundation, and thus reasserts the damnation of the heathen.

THE PLYMOUTH DECLARATION.

In the doctrinal agitation which arose with the Unitarian controversy, about thirty-four of the oldest churches in New England — comprising the greater part of the churches whose elders and messengers adopted the Boston

Confession — entirely renounced the Calvinistic system, and appealed in a larger and more generous way to New Testament Christianity, as superior to Confessional interpretations. But the Orthodox part of the Congregational body, as late as 1865, in its Declaration of Faith adopted at Plymouth, Mass., freely and gratefully accepted the "dark and awful" doctrines embodied in the Boston Confession of 1680, which was a republication of the horrors of the Savoy and Westminster confessions quoted above : —

" Standing by the rock where the Pilgrims set foot upon these shores, upon the spot where they worshipped God, and among the graves of the early generations, we, Elders and Messengers of the Congregational Churches of the United States in National Council assembled, — like them acknowledging no rule of faith but the Word of God, — do now declare our adherence to the faith and order of the apostolic and primitive churches held by our fathers, and substantially as embodied in the confessions and platforms which our Synods of 1648 and 1680 set forth or reaffirmed. We declare that the experience of the nearly two and a half centuries which have elapsed since the memorable day when our sires founded here a Christian Commonwealth, with all the development of new forms of error since their times, has only deepened our confidence in the faith and polity of those fathers. *We bless God for the inheritance of these doctrines.* We invoke the help of the Divine Redeemer that, through the presence of the promised Comforter, he will enable us to transmit *them in purity to our children.*"

Blessing God for the inheritance of a doctrine which damns the vast majority of the human race to endless woe! Praying that the Divine Redeemer would enable them to transmit these horrors in purity to their children! There are many things to be profoundly grateful for in the old Puritan heritage, but these are not a part of them. We may forgive the men of two hundred years ago for believing in mediæval superstitions; but what shall we say of those who, in all the light of our own day, reaffirm them? Their Elders and Messengers of 1865 might have found a better occasion for gratitude in the joyous consciousness that they were at liberty to correct the errors of their fathers, and to give to the Evangelical conception of Christianity a new breadth, by affirming those spiritual truths of which the Westminster Confession is but a ghastly parody. It is a pleasure, however, to record the increased influence which the Liberal minority in the Orthodox Congregational body has achieved, an influence strong enough to render the passage of the Burial Hill Declaration inexpedient to-day, if not impracticable.

CREED OF THE PARK STREET CHURCH.

Assent to the old creeds, or abridgments of them, which contain the doctrines we arraign, is still required, however, in many of the most representative Orthodox churches. The following are the articles which the pastor and deacons of Park Street Church, Boston, are required to sign : —

" *First.* We believe that the Scriptures of the Old and New Testament are the Word of GOD, and the only perfect rule of Christian faith and practice.

" *Second.* We profess our decided attachment to that system of the Christian religion which is distinguishingly denominated *Evangelical;* more particularly to those doctrines, which in a proper sense, are styled the Doctrines of Grace, viz: ' That there is one and but one living and true GOD, subsisting in three persons, the FATHER, the SON, and the HOLY GHOST; and that these Three are the one GOD, the same in substance, equal in power and glory; that GOD from all eternity, according to the counsel of His own will, and for His own glory, foreordained whatsoever comes to pass; that GOD in His most holy, wise, and powerful providence preserves and governs all His creatures and all their actions; that, by the Fall, all mankind lost communion with GOD, are under His wrath and curse, and liable to all the miseries of this life, to death itself, and to the pains of hell forever; that GOD out of His mere good pleasure, from all

eternity elected some to everlasting life, entered into a covenant
of grace, to deliver them from a state of sin and misery, and
introduce them into a state of salvation by a Redeemer; that
this Redeemer is the Lord JESUS CHRIST, the eternal Son of
GOD, who became man, and continues to be GOD and man in
two distinct natures and one person forever; that the effectual
calling of sinners is the work of GOD's Spirit; that their justification is only for the sake of CHRIST's righteousness by faith.'
And though we deem no man or body of men infallible, yet we
believe that those divines that were eminently distinguished in
the time of the Reformation, possessed the spirit, and maintained
in great purity, the peculiar doctrines of our holy religion; and
that these doctrines are in general clearly and happily expressed
in the Westminster Assembly's Shorter Catechism, and in the
Confession of Faith owned and consented unto by the Elders
and Messengers of the Churches, assembled at Boston (N. E.),
May 12th, A. D. 1680.''

The creed of Park Street Church thus asserts that " all
mankind lost communion with God, are under his wrath
and curse, and liable to all the miseries of this life, to
death itself, and to the pains of hell forever." " Some,"
we are told, " are elected to everlasting life." If we wish
to know how vast a majority of the human race are excluded from this elected "some," we turn to the Boston
Confession to which we have been referred by the Park
Street Creed itself, and read the implied damnation of
unelect infants, and the expressed damnation of the great
body of the heathen world: —

" III. *Elect* Infants dying in Infancy are Regenerated and
Saved by Christ, who worketh when and where and how he
pleaseth: So also are all other Elect Persons, who are uncapable
of being outwardly called by the Ministry of the Word."

" IV. *Others not elected*, although they may be called by the
Ministry of the Word, and may have some common Operations
of the Spirit, yet not being effectually drawn by the Father,
they neither do nor can come unto Christ, and therefore cannot
be saved; much less can these, not professing the Christian
Religion, be saved in any other way whatsoever, be they never

so diligent to frame their Lives according to the Light of Nature
and the Law of that Religion they do profess : And to assert
and maintain that they may, is very pernicious and to be
detested." (Chap. x.)

Whatever may be the personal opinions of the pastor
of Park Street Church, the creed which he is required to
subscribe teaches this "dark and awful doctrine," and we
have no doubt that there is still sung in Park Street
Church, to the doleful tune of "Windham," a hymn run-
ning : —

> "Broad is the road that leads to death,
> And thousands walk together there ;
> But wisdom shows a narrow path,
> With here and there a traveller."

Sixty years ago Prof. Andrews Norton, when engaged
in a controversy on the teachings of Calvinism, felt obliged
to say of some of his opponents : —

"Instead of endeavoring to maintain, they have denied the
doctrines of their own system. They have had the assurance
to assert that *that* was not Calvinism which for almost three centuries every theologian has known and acknowledged to be
Calvinism. They have refused, when pressed hardly, and the
occasion has required it, to acknowledge the fundamental doctrines of their own creeds and confessions and standard writers.
They have not given them up explicitly and honestly, and said
they could not defend them, but they have, in fact, denied the
Calvinistic faith, at the very moment they have been pretending
to support it, and have been reviling those by whom it was
openly opposed." — *Christian Disciple*, 1822, p. 263.

These strictures of Professor Norton are not without
their application to-day.

We have presented evidence from the principal Evangelical Creeds of Christendom, which we submit, honestly
and historically interpreted, clearly teach this doctrine of
the damnation of the majority. We could frame no blacker
indictment of Christianity than is presented in these documents ; and let it not be forgotten that they are still the
acknowledged standards of Evangelical Protestantism.

III.

The Doctrine of the Doom of the Majority still Taught by Evangelical Denominations.

Having shown that this doctrine has been alleged by Orthodoxy to be the teaching of the Scripture, and that it is taught in its authoritative standards, we purpose now to show that it is still held, taught, and urged as a practical motive by Evangelical denominations. Orthodoxy has abandoned its former belief in infant damnation, though the piteous cries of damned children still echo from the pages of its creeds. It no longer deduces that doctrine from Scripture teaching. But it has never surrendered the doctrine that the vast majority of mankind are doomed to eternal misery. The horror still appears in its literature, is still preached in its pulpits and taught in its Sunday-schools.

There are three legitimate ways of finding fairly what a denomination teaches, all of which must be employed. First, we may appeal to its standards. There are some who say, with Dr. Withrow, that this is the only proper way. Secondly, we may appeal to prominent and acknowledged representatives. That is, we may appeal, not only to its standards, but to its *standard bearers* — to the men that conduct its theological schools, train its ministers, fill its representative pulpits, and create its literature. It is necessary to compare its creeds with its current teachings. Thirdly, we may examine its practical missionary motive as well as its theoretical teaching.

We have already appealed to the standards ; and have found the doctrine we assail distinctly taught in them. Let us now appeal to its modern and representative spokesmen, and examine its practical missionary motive.

4

DR. EMMONS'S TEACHING.

We have referred before to Dr. Emmons. In the course of his long pastorate, he trained nearly a hundred students for the ministry. He was interested, too, in the formation of Andover Seminary. "Perhaps no theological instructor in the land," says Dr. Park, "has come so near as Emmons to spreading his pupils through an entire century." And what did Dr. Emmons teach his pupils, as well as the people that sat under his ministration? A few extracts will show : —

" *Though there are only a few of his people who are conformed to his image, and the great mass of mankind are opposed to his little flock, and* conspiring to destroy it, yet all that his Father has given him shall come to him." (Vol. ii. p. 386.)

" This doctrine [of reprobation] cannot be preached too plainly. It ought to be represented as God's eternal and effectual purpose to destroy the non-elect. God could not reprobate any from eternity without intending to carry his eternal purpose into execution." (Vol. ii. p. 401.)

" If the good of the intelligent creation *in general* may *sometimes* require God to give up the good of *individuals*, then it may, for aught we know, require him to give up the good of *individuals forever*. If the general good of mankind once required the temporal destruction of Pharaoh and his hosts, who knows but the *general good* of the whole intelligent creation may also require their *eternal destruction?* Therefore, allowing that God does, in this sense, aim supremely and solely at the *general* good of the intelligent creation, yet he may, nevertheless, make *myriads and myriads* of individuals finally and eternally miserable." (Vol. iii. p. 779.)

" If all are sinners in consequence of Adam's first transgression, then all have need of embracing the gospel. No other way of salvation is provided." (Vol. ii. p. 612.)

Dr. Emmons even teaches that Arminians will be included among the doomed majority.

" If God is to be justified in his treatment of Pharaoh and of all the rest of the non-elect, then it is *absolutely necessary to approve of the doctrine of reprobation in order to be saved.* None can be admitted to heaven who are not prepared to join in the employments as well as the enjoyments of the heavenly world. And we know that one part of the business of the blessed is to celebrate the doctrine of reprobation. They sing the Song of Moses and the Lamb, which is an anthem of praise for the destruction of Pharaoh and his reprobate host. How, then, can any be meet for an inheritance among the saints in light, who are not reconciled to the doctrine of reprobation, which is, and which will be forever, celebrated there?" (Vol. ii. p. 402.)

According to this view, Methodists, and Arminians among all the denominations, stand a poor chance.

Dr. Emmons also shows that character and good works will not avail in the slightest : —

"We learn from what has been said why none of the works of sinners will be accepted at the last day. Our Saviour, who will be the final Judge, has absolutely declared that he will condemn all sinners and all their works without distinction in the great day of account. And though they may plead that they have fed the hungry, clothed the naked, visited the sick, and done many deeds of apparent humanity and benevolence, yet he will reject and punish them for that criminal selfishness which was the source of all their actions. And this will be a sufficient reason for their everlasting perdition." (Vol. ii. p. 644.)

Dr. Emmons further shows that God created men especially to damn them for his good pleasure : —

"Now, if God be capable of great and noble designs, if he be capable of great and noble exertions, and capable of taking a true, real, infinite pleasure and delight in all his works, then it is easy to conceive that he might make his own pleasure, his own blessedness or glory, the grand and supreme object in all his works of creation and providence, and have but an inferior and subordinate respect to the good of the creature. Accordingly, the Scripture represents this as his ultimate and supreme end in the creation of the world. 'The Lord hath made all things for himself; yea, even the wicked for the day of evil.'" (*The Process of the General Judgment*, Works, vol. iii., p. 780.)

These are the teachings which the Congregational Publication Society republishes in 1860.

DR. ENOCH POND'S TEACHING.

Let us take another Orthodox theological school, that at Bangor, Me., and turn to the teachings of its venerable and respected president, Rev. Enoch Pond, D.D., who died in January, 1882. In an article on "The Future of the Heathen," in the *Christian Review*, Dr. Pond writes with the terrible earnestness of one who accepts the logical consequences of this doctrine, and whose spirit of benevolence is stirred to the depths for the relief of the damned.

" The conclusion, therefore, remains unshaken, notwithstanding all the objections which may be urged against it, that *the end of heathenism is eternal death*, and that the *great body of* the *adult heathen* (for we believe that infants are saved the world over) will lose their souls forever.

" And now, what a dreadful conclusion is this! Let us pause and ponder it, and not be in haste to dismiss it from our minds. Not less than six hundred millions of the present inhabitants of our globe are heathens. Three fourths of this number are adult heathens. Each one of these is an immortal creature, destined to outlive the stars, destined to exist forever.

" Now they have a season of probation; but this is rapidly and, in respect to successive multitudes of them, constantly coming to a close. A mighty stream is ever pouring them over the boundaries of time; and, when once they have passed these boundaries, where do they fall? Alas! we have seen where! They fall to rise no more. They sink in darkness, misery, and despair. They go to be treated not hardly or cruelly, but *justly ;* go to Him by whom " actions are weighed; " go to be punished as their sins deserve, forever. Now these are not fictions, but *facts*, — facts fully established by the Scriptures, and proved incontestably in the preceding remarks. And are they not stunning, overwhelming facts, — sufficient, and more than sufficient, to rouse up every Christian's heart?

" Here is a broad current rushing downward from the heathen world into that lake which burneth with unquenchable fire, on which hundreds of millions of immortal beings are descending, and by which thousands upon thousands are every day destroyed;

and shall we sit down and contemplate such a scene, shall we be able to speak and write about it unmoved ? Or shall not each one rather exclaim, in accents prompted by Christian love: —

> 'My God, I *feel* the mournful scene !
> My spirits yearn o'er dying men !
> And fain my pity would reclaim,
> And snatch the firebrands from the flame.' "

(*Christian Review*, vol. xxii. 1857, p. 41.)

DR. SHEDD'S TEACHING.

There is also an Orthodox theological seminary at New York, and Dr. W. G. T. Shedd is one of its eminent professors. In a sermon delivered before the Presbyterian Board of Foreign Missions, May 3, 1863, entitled "The Guilt of the Pagan," and published by the American Board in 1864, Dr. Shedd says : —

"Unless the *guilt* of the pagan world can be proved, the missionary enterprises of the Christian church, from the days of the Apostles to the present time, have all been a waste of labor." (p. 1.)

"It follows inevitably from these positions of St. Paul concerning the guilt of the pagan, that *nothing but revealed religion can save him from an eternity of sin and woe.*" (p. 21.)

"Our Lord and Saviour knew infallibly how many *millions upon millions* of the race for whom he proposed to pour out his life-blood would reject him. He knew long beforehand how *many millions upon millions of this miserable and infatuated race* would resist and ultimately quench the only Spirit that could renovate and save them." (p. 23.)

"It is this dark and awful fact," says Dr. Shedd in closing his sermon, — dark and awful it truly seems, — "that the Church of Christ is continually to keep in mind." (p. 22.) The Prudential Committee of the American Board were so impressed with the force of this argument that they directed a copy of the sermon to be sent to the pastors of the various churches which contribute to the treasury of the American Board. The secretary, Rev. S. B. Treat, indorsing his position, says, " *The entire heathen world is guilty, condemned, lost.*" (The Italics are his.) This is still the position of the American Board. It bases its appeals on this "dark and awful fact." Dr. Edwards A. Park, at the great missionary meeting in Portland, in October, 1882, and in a subsequent discourse, took substantially the same position, and asserted that the missionary nerve would be cut if a probation after death were allowed to the heathen.

REV. ALBERT BARNES, D. D.

Rev. Albert Barnes was a leading preacher and writer in the Presbyterian Church. In the following passage from one of his sermons the great majority of mankind are excluded from all hope of heaven : —

" The admission that the Christian religion is true is a condemnation of all other systems, and shuts out all who are not interested in the plan of the gospel from all hope of heaven." (*The Way of Salvation*, p. 12.)

As we shall see further on, Dr. Barnes struggled hard with the terrible mystery of this doctrine.

REV. A. A. HODGE, D. D.

Dr. A. A. Hodge of Princeton Theological Seminary, in his Commentary on the Confession of Faith (1869), admits without a sign of hesitancy the damnation of the majority.

" That the diligent profession and honest practice of neither *natural religion, nor of any other religion than pure Christianity* can in the least avail to promote the salvation of the soul, is evident from the essential principles of the gospel." (*Commentary on Conf.*, p. 241.)

" That in the case of sane adult persons a knowledge of Christ and a voluntary acceptance of him is essential in order to a personal interest in his salvation is proved — (1) Paul argues this point explicitly : If men call upon the Lord they shall be saved; but in order to call upon him they must believe; and in order to believe they must hear; and that they should hear the gospel must be preached unto them. . . . (2) God has certainly revealed no purpose to save any except those who, hearing the gospel, obey; and he requires that his people, as custodians of the gospel, should be diligent in disseminating it as the appointed means of saving souls. Whatever lies beyond this circle of sanctified means is unrevealed, unpromised, uncovenanted. (3) The heathen in mass, with no single definite and unquestionable exception on record, are evidently strangers to God, and are going down to death in an unsaved condition. The presumed possibility of being saved without a knowledge of Christ remains, after eighteen hundred years, a possibility illustrated by no example." (*Ib.*, p. 242.)

How Dr. Hodge obtained this information, he does not tell us. It presumes a familiarity with God's judgments, which perhaps is granted only to the elect.

PRINCETON REVIEW.

Dr. Hodge's views on this point are confirmed by an article in the *Princeton Review*, the authoritative organ of the Seminary, published in 1860, and entitled "The Heathen Inexcusable for their Idolatry." [1]

" They who have never known of a Saviour cannot be guilty of the sin of rejecting him. What then is the ground of their condemnation? This question is an important one; for, if the heathen are not under condemnation, what is the use of sending them the gospel? If the heathen, or the greater portion of them, are to get to heaven through their ignorance, where is the necessity for any clearer light, which, reasoning from all past experience, the greater majority will not receive? The question, in fact, lies still further back, as to the necessity of any gospel at all. If we, or any single individual man, could have been saved without the atonement, then righteousness would have been by that method, and Christ would not have died. The gospel,

---

[1] In Poole's Index the writer's name is given as J. K. Wight.

however, looks upon all as in a state of condemnation, and that none can hope for justification and eternal life except through the righteousness of Christ alone." (*Princeton Review*, 1860, vol. xxxii. p. 427.)

"The heathen are under condemnation, and to them a dark and hopeless one: they know of no escape. While, therefore, their sin is far less than of those who know the remedy and reject it, still their condition is one which should excite our deepest pity and compassion. The wrath of God is abiding on them. From the second death, and all its terrors, they know of no escape; but to us the only remedy for them and us has been made known. It is not our object to dwell upon the practical conclusion which the apostle draws from the fact that the heathen are under condemnation; but the more we recognize the fact, the more important must we feel to be the inference from it, — namely, that the only hope for Jew and Gentile is in justification through faith in Christ, that his is the only name given under heaven whereby men can be saved." (*Ib.*, p. 448.)

The damnation of the heathen has not only been held as a theological tenet, but it has been urged as the great practical motive for missionary effort. This is strikingly evident in the article of Dr. Enoch Pond, already quoted. In preparing this treatise we have examined all the sermons which have been preached before the American Board of Commissioners for Foreign Missions during the last forty years, and a few delivered before that Board was formed.

We have been impressed in these sermons with the earnestness, zeal, piety, faith, hope, and love which they express, and the ability with which they have been prepared. The range of minor motives, minor when viewed from the Orthodox standpoint, is considerable. The good effect of missionary work on the churches themselves, the improvement of the temporal condition of the heathen, the encouragements derived from work already done, are from time to time presented. There are sermons which are marked by a pessimistic tone, in which the miseries of the heathen now and hereafter are pictured; and there are sermons thoroughly optimistic in their belief in the final triumph of Christianity. Indeed, it has ever been a powerful motive in missionary appeal to paint the millennial glories of an entire world converted to Jesus Christ. Sometimes, love to Christ is presented as a constraining motive; sometimes, the *duty* of the Church to obey his command to preach his gospel to all nations. Less frequently than either of these, though often urged with tenderness and power, are the obligations that spring from human brotherhood. Some writers find their inspiration in the great number of the heathen that will be saved if the gospel is sent; others in the vast number that will be lost if it is not sent.

But — whatever be the minor motives which give variety, ingenuity, and force to these yearly appeals — the underlying premise on which they are all built is the assumption that the heathen form part of a lost and ruined world, and that nothing but a personal acceptance of the gospel of Jesus Christ can save them from eternal misery. This is the key-note of the earliest and latest of these discourses. It is the corner-stone of the missionary power. A few extracts from some of these sermons, and other missionary literature, will show the tenacity with which this doctrine is held, and how vital it has been deemed to the whole system.

REV. GORDON HALL.

Rev. Gordon Hall, a missionary, in a sermon preached in 1812, in Philadelphia, said : —

"While the whole number of souls now upon the globe amounts to no less than eight hundred millions, there are by computation five hundred millions who have never heard of the name of Jesus, who know not that a Savior has bled for sinners, and are *rushing through pagan darkness by millions down to hopeless death.*" (p. 4.)

"The poor pagans have not a ray of gospel light to guide them to the world of glory. They are by millions perishing for lack of those precious privileges which so many in this country are abusing to their own damnation." (p. 15.)

REV. MYRON WINSLOW.

At a meeting held at the Old South Church, Boston, June 7, 1819, on the evening previous to the sailing of several missionaries to Ceylon, Rev. Myron Winslow said : —

"It cannot be denied that the general representation of the Bible concerning the heathen world is that they are going down to perdition. If, still, the thought of such vast multitudes sinking into hell, without any knowledge of the only name given under heaven by which they can be saved, seems inconsistent with the goodness of God, we are to remember that they, with all our fallen race, *deserve* eternal misery; that the provisions of the gospel are wholly gratuitous, God being under no obligation to communicate them to any; and, if not to any, certainly not to all; that he has a right to choose whom he will to salvation; and, if he leaves whole nations to *perish*, it is right. . . . It is true, the heathen are to be judged according to the light they have: they cannot be condemned for rejecting a salvation which was never offered them; but they *may* be condemned, they *will* be condemned, for putting out the light of nature." (p. 12.)

REV. WILLIAM HERVEY.

Rev. William Hervey, missionary to India, 1829, said : —

"Brethren, have the terms of admission to heaven been altered since they were laid down by the Saviour ? Have the requisitions of the gospel been softened since the days of the apostles ? I know that many professors feel and act as though this was the case. But heaven and earth shall pass away before one human sinner shall be admitted to glory on altered terms."

MISS MARY LYON.

Miss Mary Lyon, the founder of South Hadley Seminary, pleaded warmly, in her " Missionary Offering " (1843), for the lost heathen : —

"The price of their redemption has been paid. The Holy Spirit has been given. But one thing more of all the counsels of heaven is wanting to secure their salvation, to make sure of their eternal safety. This one thing is the voluntary instrumentality of man. For the want of this, *millions and millions* during the last eighteen centuries have gone down to everlasting death." (p. 30.)

REV. THOMAS H. SKINNER, D. D.

Rev. Thomas H. Skinner, D.D., of New York, preached the sermon in 1843, and lays down what he considers some essential facts on this point: —

" In the Christian scheme, the following facts are essential : that mankind are in a state of sin, and dying in this state are utterly lost; that their recovery can be effected *only by their being Christianized or brought under the power of the gospel; that the gospel can do nothing where it has not been propagated or is unknown.*" (p. 7.)

In another passage of the same sermon, Dr. Skinner shows how negligent the Church has been in evangelizing the world, and to give effect to his reproach adds an interesting calculation : —

" Never, since the primitive era, has she [the Church] given indication that she felt herself under the sanction of any authority to evangelize the nations of the earth, while *by twenty millions a year, during eighteen centuries,* they have been passing to their eternal destiny, strangers to the influence of God's recovering grace." (p. 11.)

REV. MARK HOPKINS, D. D.

Rev. Dr. Hopkins, in his sermon in 1845, considered humanitarian and civilizing influences alone as insufficient to meet the need of the heathen, and said : —

" The burden which rests upon us is not simply a proclamation of the gospel among the heathen, but such a proclamation of it as *shall save the soul.* If we fail of this, we fail of our object altogether." (p. 19.)

REV. FRANCIS BOWMAN.

In a missionary sermon by Rev. Francis Bowman (Presbyterian), preached in 1846, we read: —

" There is not in all truth anything so important to be known by the whole world as the fact that ' Christ Jesus came into the world to save sinners.' Impart all other truth, yet, if this be withheld, the *teeming millions of the earth's population will perish.*" (p. 7.)

REV. RUFUS ANDERSON, D.D.

Rev. Dr. Rufus Anderson, senior secretary of the American Board, said in 1851: —

" Nothing is more truly binding upon us than the obligation to impart the gospel to those whom we can reach, and who *will perish if they do not receive it.* That, surely, is the most destructive immorality which withholds from immortal man the only gospel of salvation. The most pernicious infidelity is surely that which cares not for a world perishing in sin." (p. 21.)

REV. GEORGE W. BETHUNE, D.D.

Rev. Dr. George W. Bethune, of the Dutch Reformed Church, urged, in 1856, the Calvinistic theology as the very basis for all missionary work as against all more liberal methods. Dr. Bethune argued that the glory belonged to Christ: —

" Even if *it were possible* (a monstrous supposition) to make men repent by any method of our own device, *we should not dare to use it;* for then we should take the praise from him, and break our loyalty. . . . The world is to be saved, but through the conversion of individual sinners. We may preach to the multitude, but *only he who by the grace of God believes the word* will be blessed." (p. 18.)

" *Myriads of our fellow-sinners,* in our land and other lands, are still in these horrible depths: the *gospel* alone can lift them out." (p. 38.)

REV. W. W. PATTON.

In an article entitled, " The True Theory of Missions to the Heathen," in the *Bibliotheca Sacra,* for July, 1858,

Rev. W. W. Patton testifies to the prevalent evangelical belief, though he does not hold it : —

" We come now to a second theory of missions, which may be called the extreme evangelical theory. . . . Can a heathen be saved who has lived and died without hearing of Jesus Christ, or of the one living and true God ? The theory which we are now to consider answers in the negative. It teaches that man can in no way be pardoned without specific faith in the Lord Jesus Christ as the Saviour of sinners ; and that all the heathen who have not been visited by the missionaries of the cross, have descended, generation after generation, in unbroken ranks, to perdition, their case having been through life as hopeless as that of men seized with a fatal malady, the only cure for which is on the other side of the globe, with no means of obtaining it. To what extent this theory is actually held, in all its rigidity, we are unable to say. It is the accepted theory of the Romish Church, and of a part of the Protestant Church, perhaps of the majority of the latter. The ordinary language of missionary letters, addresses, sermons, and reports implies or favors this extreme view." (*Bibliotheca Sacra*, vol. xv. p. 552.)

Mr. Patton might have gone further, and said that this missionary literature not only implies or favors this extreme view, but that it continually asserts it as absolutely necessary to the missionary motive. But we have later and additional testimony on this point.

REV. R. W. PATTERSON, D. D.

Rev. Dr. Patterson, of the Second Presbyterian Church, Chicago, said, in 1859 : —

" Remember! All these thousands and millions who are living and dying without the gospel are of your own blood ! Remember! Their souls are as precious as yours ; Jesus died for them as well as for you. Remember! They are going on rapidly to the same great Eternity which lies before you; and what you do for them must be done quickly. I tell you, my brethren, we are strong in our cause, when we can press motives like these upon the hearts of all the multitudes who know how to feel for the woes of perishing souls." (p. 16.)

The sermon of Dr. Shedd on the "Guilt of the Pagan," published in 1864, has already been referred to. An additional quotation is in place here:—

"Natural religion consigns the entire pagan world to eternal perdition. . . . It is precisely because the pagan world has not obeyed the principles of natural religion, and is under a curse and a bondage therefor, that it is in perishing need of the truths of revealed religion. Little do those know what they are saying, when they propose to find a salvation for the pagan in the mere light of natural reason and conscience." (pp. 20, 21.)

REV. E. N. KIRK, D. D.

Rev. Dr. Kirk of Boston said, in 1865:—

"The increase of the world's population marches with gigantic strides. More pagans *are born*, more *die in one year, than we have converted in over fifty years.*" (p. 19.)

This shows how few heathen are saved, compared with the number that are lost. This calculation of Dr. Kirk may be compared with that of Dr. Skinner.

REV. GEORGE H. POND.

Rev. George H. Pond, a Presbyterian clergyman and a missionary in Minnesota, in an article in the *Presbyterian Quarterly Review*, January, 1861, said:—

"The millions of those who compose the churches believe, or profess to believe, that the teachings of the Bible are the teachings of God. They profess to believe that *the man is lost in sin, that Jesus toiled and died to save him, and that nothing else can save him except the provisions of the gospel.* [Italics are his.] . . . And yet, notwithstanding all this profession, pagans may be counted by tens and by hundreds of millions, who have not even heard the name of Jesus. Hundreds of millions have not a solitary friend to point them to the Lamb of God, to the blood of the atonement."

President Fairchild of Oberlin College, in 1877, was very clear on this point:—

" The great masses of mankind have no such knowledge of God as affords them any help or hope for this life or that which is to come. . . . Enough of light is mingled with the darkness to give the sense of duty and the consciousness of sin,— not enough to awaken hope or move them to effort for a better life. They belong to the kingdom of darkness, and the powers of darkness hold them in bondage. . . . There are none who, by special strength or courage, lift themselves above this degradation, and walk in ways of righteousness and in the light of God. Thus in darkness and sin great masses of our fellow-men live and die, and thus they have lived and died throughout the history of the race. . . . Our brother of India, of China, of Africa, is perishing within our reach and before our eyes. Can we go our various ways, one to his farm, and another to his merchandise, and not incur the final condemnation, ' Inasmuch as ye did it not to one of the least of these, ye did it not to me '?" (pp. 9, 17.)

In no sermon delivered before the American Board has this doctrine of the perishing condition of the heathen received more distinct utterance than in the sermon before that body, delivered by Rev. Dr. E. P. Goodwin of Chicago, at Portland, Oct. 3, 1882. This sermon has special significance because delivered at a time when the question of a second probation for the heathen was actively discussed in the Orthodox Congregational body. Dr. Goodwin holds that all lax doctrine is hostile to the missionary spirit, and plants himself firmly on the old theological foundation:—

" This missionary gospel, this gospel to be preached among all the nations, was to be emphatically a *gospel of separation*, a gospel of election, a gospel everywhere calling out and setting apart a peculiar people. . . . In other words, the supreme end which in this age the Holy Spirit proposes to accomplish by this witnessing of the gospel to all nations, is to call out thence a people chosen in Christ Jesus before the foundation of the world." (p. 7.)

Dr. Goodwin then shows how few in number the elect are : —

" We stand under the pierced hands and the bleeding side. We know this cross over our heads means blood shed, death suffered, for the sin of the world. We compass the nations and the ages in our thought, and with him that hangs here our hearts reach out far and wide with ardent desire, with inexpressible and tearful longings, that all men may know this Christ, may accept this gospel, may possess eternal life.

" But *God's desires are not God's decrees.* This Christ pitying all, eager to save all, is the Christ rejected, hated, crucified, by those he seeks to save. The amazing invitation, ' Come unto me, all ye that labor and are heavy-laden, and I will give you rest,' is uttered in all ears ; but only here and there a Nicodemus, a woman at the well, a thief on the cross, makes response. Across the continents, for eighteen centuries, have sounded the wonderful words, ' God so loved the world that he gave his only begotten Son, that whosoever believeth in him should not perish, but have everlasting life ;' but, among the *swarming millions, how insignificant the numbers that care to listen, and how few of these that are eager to possess the gift!* " (p. 8.)

Dr. Goodwin is amazed that so few should accept the gospel : —

" Are any now oppressed with the thought that this conception of the missionary work makes it seem a kind of hopeless undertaking ? Do they stand facing these unsaved millions, and, with a feeling almost of dismay, ask why, after eighteen centuries of the preaching of the cross, so few *comparatively have been reached and saved !* I do not wonder. There are mysteries here that no human wisdom can solve." (p. 10.)

MISSIONARY REPORTS.

The American Board of Commissioners for Foreign Missions says : —

"To send the gospel to the heathen is a work of great exigency. Within the last thirty years, a whole generation of five hundred millions have gone down to eternal death."

Again the same Board, in its tract entitled "The Grand Motive to Missionary Effort," written by one of the secretaries of the Board and published in 1853, says: —

"Another and a very powerful motive in this enterprise is found in the *awful doom which awaits those who live and die within the precincts of pagan idolatry.* [Italics theirs.] This great fact, clearly recognized in the Scriptures, is fitted to rouse the deepest sympathies of the soul. No believer in Christianity can imagine that Christ would have directed his followers to send the gospel to 'every creature,' at such a vast expense of toil and treasure and suffering and blood, to be continued down through the lapse of ages, if he had known or supposed that the heathen could and would be saved just as well without the gospel as with it. No theory which admits idolaters of any description into the kingdom of heaven can be reconciled with the facts and teachings of the Bible. The heathen are involved in the ruins of the apostasy, are subjects of a deep and awful depravity, totally unfit for heaven, and are expressly doomed to perdition. No body of men denying this doctrine ever undertook to evangelize the dark places of the earth; and it may well be doubted whether they ever will. Here, then, we have before us a great truth, a Bible truth, fitted to fix the eye and pierce the heart.

'The heathen perish; day by day,
Thousands on thousands pass away.'

"If the Christians of this land could stand together on some eminence near the gates of Eternity, and see the sweeping torrent of deathless souls, from the realms of paganism, daily and hourly passing through, and plunging into the fathomless depths below, what eye would not run down with tears? what bosom would not heave with emotion? what heart would not be transfixed with agonies? what tongue would not pray and cry aloud to God, that this river of death might be stopped? . . . A deathless soul, on the brink of hell, with capacities for heaven, and full provision made for its salvation! What a spectacle!

5

Multiply this one by six hundred millions and then contemplate the scene." (pp. 7, 8.)

Bishop Colenso, in his "Ten Weeks in Natal," gives the following extract from an American missionary report : —

"Every hour, yea, every moment they are dying, and dying, most of them, without any knowledge of the Saviour. On whom now rests the responsibility? If you fail to do all in your power to save them, will you stand at the judgment guiltless of their blood? Said a heathen child, after having embraced the Gospel, to the writer, ' How long have they had the Gospel in New England?' When told, she asked, with great earnestness, ' Why did they not come and tell us this before?' and then added, ' My mother died, and my father died, and my brother died, without the Gospel.' Here she was unable to restrain her emotions. But, at length, wiping away her tears, she asked, ' Where do you think they have gone?' I, too, could not refrain from weeping, and, turning to her, I inquired, ' Where do *you* think they have gone?' She hesitated a few moments, and then replied, with much emotion, ' I suppose they have gone down to the dark place — the dark place. Oh! why did they not tell us before?' It wrung my heart as she repeated the question, ' Why did they not tell us before?'"

What shall we say of the gladness of a gospel which carries such tidings to ignorant heathen? Remarking on this passage the *North British Review* says : —

" Can this be mere *ad captandum* language, intended to draw contributions to the missionary societies? If so, it is very wicked. But if it be really genuine and sincere, how melancholy a fanaticism does it display! We shudder at the accounts of Devil-worship which come to us from so many mission-fields. We pity the dreary delusion of the Manichees, who enthroned the Evil Principle in heaven. But if we proclaim that God is indeed one who could decree this more than Moloch sacrifice *of the vast majority of his own creatures and children,* for no fault or sin of theirs, we revive the error of the Manichees; for the God whom we preach as the destroyer of the guiltless can be no God of justice, far less a God of love." (Vol. xxv. Aug. 1856, p. 317.)

IV.

ADMISSIONS AND CRITICISMS.

IN the foregoing pages we have presented an array of unimpeachable evidence concerning the authoritative, traditional, and current Evangelical belief in regard to this "dark and awful doctrine." We have examined the most prevalent Orthodox interpretations of Scripture; we have appealed to the standards of Orthodoxy, and to the men who made them, — to its theological seminaries, its missionary bodies, its authoritative literature, the teachings of its pulpits. And now we ask, What becomes of the statement that "no Orthodox denomination, no Evangelical creed in Christendom, teaches that the vast majority of the human race are to be the victims of endless woe"?

In the light — or, more fitly, in the gloom — of this mass of testimony, we appeal to the candor of our readers whether it is an "absolute and abominable misrepresentation" of Orthodoxy to say that it has taught and still teaches the hideous doctrine of the eternal damnation of the majority of the race? If anybody has misrepresented Orthodoxy in this respect, it is not we who report its utterances, but John Calvin, Richard Baxter, Matthew Henry, a host of Evangelical commentators, the Synod of Dort, the makers of the Westminster, the Savoy, and the Boston confessions, the American Tract Society, the American and Presbyterian Boards of Foreign Missions, and the great leaders of Orthodox theological schools. We admit that the word *misrepresentation* may be applied to the awful doctrine which has been described, but it is as a misrepresentation of Christianity, not of Orthodoxy.

We do not claim that this unnatural doctrine has never met with protest. On the contrary, through all the years in which it has been taught, — under the shelter of Biblical, Papal, and Synodical authority, — there have been men who have lifted up their voices against it, from the time of Origen down to Murray, Chapin, Bellows, and Farrar. But they have always been in the minority, and have either been cast out of organized Orthodoxy, or regarded with suspicion. When Curio, in 1532, maintained that "the number of the saved, in which he includes virtuous heathen, will far exceed that of the lost, this doctrine was deemed so dangerous that the Senate of Basel refused to allow him to publish the work, and the first edition was printed surreptitiously."[1] We honor the brave souls in every age who have protested against the moral and practical implications of this belief, and wish there was no longer any occasion to continue their remonstrance; but in spite of the increasing minority of those who have repudiated it within Orthodox circles, we are forced, after a wide examination of current testimony, to the conclusion of Canon Farrar, that "it is needless to prove that this has continued to be the popular opinion."[2]

1. Evangelical Admissions.

That an Orthodox minister in Boston should indignantly deny that " any Evangelical creed in Christendom " teaches the doom of the majority, may be construed as a virtual admission that the doctrine is not one which Orthodoxy would gladly own. There is another line of defence

---

[1] For references concerning those who have taken ground in behalf of the salvability of the unconverted heathen, and in fact for the general and special literature of every aspect of the doctrine of the future life, see the Bibliography by Professor Ezra Abbot, D.D., LL.D., of Harvard University, appended to Rev. W. R. Alger's " Critical History of the Doctrine of a Future Life." No one can treat any phase of this subject historically without consulting this invaluable Bibliography. In addition to the constant aid we have obtained from it, we must also acknowledge the kind assistance of its author in revising proofs of these pages.

[2] Mercy and Judgment, p. 154.

open to persons of this view, and that is, to show that modern Orthodoxy has renounced the tenets of Calvin, the Westminster Assembly, the Synod of Dort, the Savoy Declaration, the Boston Confession, the Plymouth Declaration, and the teachings of Emmons, Pond, Park, Hodge, and the numerous authorities we have quoted. Liberal Orthodoxy has taken a step in this direction, but the great majority of the Orthodox, Congregational, Presbyterian, Baptist, and Reformed denominations are not yet ready to confess that the Creeds and Fathers were mistaken in this matter. On the contrary, the doctrine is still freely and boldly confessed. It is even considered dangerous to Orthodoxy to relax in any degree its rigorous belief in respect to the destiny of the great body of the heathen world.

VARIOUS LETTERS.

Since the appearance of our article on this subject in the *Christian Register* of Jan. 4, 1883, we have received various communications from Orthodox believers who have expressed their surprise that the prevalence of the doctrine should be at all questioned.

A lady, whose goodness is as sound as her Orthodoxy, writes concerning the doom of the majority: —

" All I will try to say is this: the doctrine is truly an awful one ; but we find it in the Bible, and those of us who believe in that book cannot ignore it. So we seek to leave the matter with Him who is not only the Judge of all the earth, but a God of infinite mercy and love. Surely, He will do that which is right."

An Orthodox minister writes: —

" It is wasting powder to prove that Orthodox Christians believe that ' broad is the way that leads to death, and many there be that walk therein;' while *strait, narrow, few*, &c., are the words of Jesus. Your quotations are perfectly fair, as proving this to be our historic and present belief. It is undoubtedly the opinion of most Orthodox Christians that the great majority of the human race, who have as yet died in mature years, are lost."

Various friends, who like the writer were reared within the Evangelical fold, have confessed that they never thought of entertaining any other belief on this subject.

THE EXAMINER.

The *Examiner*, of New York, is one of the most prominent organs of the Baptist denomination in this country. In a comparatively recent issue, it freely concedes the point we have pressed, in regard to the damnation of the vast majority of the adult portion of the race. It says: —

" The idea of a probation in this life does imply the possibility of salvation, but the possibility may never be realized. As a matter of fact, we believe that, for *the vast majority of the heathen, this possibility never is realized, and we never yet heard of an Orthodox theologian who held any other belief than this.*" [1]

This is a sad confession to make, but it has the virtue of candor.

THE PRESBYTERIAN.

The doctrine is again frankly acknowledged in an editorial article in the *Presbyterian*, March 10, 1883. It is considered to be absolutely essential to the missionary motive: —

" Foreign Missions were conceived in the idea that the heathen world was perishing, and that the duty of the Church was, by every sacrifice possible, to save them. Any such scheme would have been still-born without this vital centre, this heart of all endeavor. The Church in New England grew strong in this conviction, — unselfish, aggressive, and glorious. The pulsations of the New England — we might say Boston — heart went to the extremities of this whole country.

" And now, after building a kingdom of power and glory at home, and laying the foundations of revolution from heathenism to new life in every nation under heaven, on which the superstructure of life eternal may go up in divine proportions, it is

---

[1] Examiner, New York, Feb. 15, 1883.

suddenly discovered in Boston that the heart has dropped out; and it must, of course, be given up.

" Foreign Mission zeal and endeavor, together, form the test of a standing or falling Church. Where there is no zeal and no conscientious sacrifice for Foreign Missions, there will be none for Home Evangelization. Hence, when this conception of urgency and sacrifice to achieve its end, because the world without salvation by Christ is dead, is abandoned, the death of Evangelism will have no geographical bounds. It will be death at home and abroad. It is a short cut to atheism, when death will reign supreme; for Home and Foreign Missions, resting on the fact given in Revelation, that the world without salvation is lost, are as supplemental to each other as the lobes of the brain, and in their workings as active and reactive."

It would be strange indeed, if, in the mass of testimony we have adduced in illustration of this doctrine, there should not be confessions of its dismal and terrible nature. The reason and the emotions must at times revolt against the hideous consequences of a dogma so painful to the affections and so contrary to our highest conceptions of divine goodness. With such an admission this paper began. Dr. Shedd confesses it to be a "dark and awful doctrine." John Calvin called it "a dreadful decree;" Chrysostom, "a terrible truth;" Doddridge, "a dreadful truth;" Dean Goulburn describes it as "awfully startling;" Rev. Enoch Pond termed it "an affecting truth, . . . a dreadful conclusion, . . . sufficient to rouse up every Christian's heart." The same confession is frankly and even tearfully made in a host of missionary discourses. Sometimes the consciousness of the painful nature of this doctrine is so poignant that we scarcely know whom to pity more, the "vast majority" condemned to this woe, or the minority, unfortunate enough to believe in their damnation.

A REMARKABLE CONFESSION.

The mysterious and appalling features of this dogma have seldom been stated with more power than by one

of the most widely known and most popular of Presbyterian preachers and commentators, Rev. Albert Barnes.[1]
Struggling with the doubts and difficulties which his
attempt to believe in this doctrine inevitably suggested,
he makes the following remarkable confession : —

"That the immortal mind should be allowed to jeopard its
infinite welfare, and that trifles should be allowed to draw it
away from God and virtue and Heaven; that any should suffer
forever, — lingering on in hopeless despair and rolling amidst
infinite torments, without the possibility of alleviation and without end; that since God *can* save men, and *will* save a part, he
has not purposed to save *all;* that, on the supposition that the
atonement is ample, and that the blood of Christ can cleanse
from all and every sin, it is not in fact applied to all; that, in a
word, a God who claims to be worthy of the confidence of the
universe, and to be a being of infinite benevolence, should make
such a world as this, full of sinners and sufferers; and that
when an atonement had been made, He did not save *all* the race,
and put an end to sin and woe forever, — these, and kindred
difficulties, meet the mind when we think on this great subject;
and they meet us when we endeavor to urge our fellow-sinners
to be reconciled to God, and to put confidence in Him. On this
ground they hesitate. These are *real*, not imaginary difficulties.
They are probably felt by every mind that has ever reflected on
the subject; and they are *unexplained*, *unmitigated*, *unremoved*.
I confess, for one, that I feel them, and feel them more sensibly
and powerfully the more I look at them, and the longer I live.
I do not understand these facts ; and I make no advances towards
understanding them. I do not know that I have a ray of light
on this subject, which I had not when the subject first flashed
across my soul.

"I have read, to some extent, what wise and good men have
written; I have looked at their theories and explanations, I have
endeavored to weigh their arguments; for my whole soul pants
for light and relief on these questions. But I get neither; and
in the distress and anguish of my own spirit, I confess that I
see no light whatever. I see not one ray to disclose to me the

---

[1] "Practical Sermons," pp. 123–125, quoted in C. F. Hudson's
"Debt and Grace," pp. 54, 55.

reason why sin came into the world, why the earth is strewed with the dying and the dead, and why man must suffer to all eternity.

" I have never yet seen a particle of light thrown on these subjects, that has given a moment's ease to my tortured mind; nor have I an explanation to offer, or a thought to suggest, that would be of relief to you. I trust other men — as they profess to do — understand this better than I do, and that they have not the anguish of spirit which I have; but I confess, when I look on a world of sinners and sufferers, upon death-beds and grave-yards, upon the world of woe, filled with hosts to suffer forever; when I see my friends, my parents, my family, my people, my fellow-citizens, — when I look upon a whole race, all involved in this sin and danger; and when I see the great mass of them wholly unconcerned, and when I feel that God only can save them, and yet he does not do it, — I am struck dumb. It is all *dark, dark, dark* to my soul, and I cannot disguise it."

There is something mournfully pathetic in such a confession as this. It reminds us that the tenets of Calvinism, even with the discriminations which they make in favor of those who accept them, are not held by tender and humane believers without pain and struggle of soul. Again we ask, can this be the natural and proper effect of the glad gospel of " peace on earth, good-will to men"? There are many sources of doubt and mystery in the world about us. It is the office of religion, truly interpreted, to help us to meet them with manly hope and faith, and not to create, from traditional and legendary assumptions, artificial mysteries which are more distressing than those which are real. Dr. Barnes here assumes, in accordance with the standards of his church, that "the whole race" is "involved in this sin and danger, and that "the *great mass of them*" will not be saved from eternal ruin, although God might do it if he wished. Is it any wonder that he says "it is all dark, dark, dark," and confesses that he has never " seen a particle of light thrown on these subjects, that has given a moment's ease to [his] tortured mind "?

A STUBBORN AND AWFUL FACT.

In the first volume of his scholarly work on "The Creeds of Christendom," Dr. Philip Schaff, in criticising the Westminster system of doctrine, candidly admits "the stubborn and awful facts" which confront it, and the difficulties that inhere not only in Calvinism, but in all other Orthodox systems : —

"It must in fairness be admitted that the Calvinistic system only traces undeniable facts to their first ante-mundane cause in the inscrutable counsel of God. It draws the legitimate logical conclusions from such anthropological and eschatological premises as are acknowledged by all other Orthodox churches, Greek, Roman, Lutheran, and Reformed. They all teach the condemnation of the human race in consequence of Adam's fall, and confine the opportunity and possibility of salvation from sin and perdition to this present life. And yet everybody must admit that the *vast majority of mankind*, no worse by nature than the rest, and without personal guilt, are born and grow up in heathen darkness, out of the reach of the means of grace, and are thus, as far as we know, actually 'passed by' in this world. *No orthodox system can logically reconcile this stubborn and awful fact with the universal love and impartial justice of God."* (*Creeds of Christendom,* vol. i. p. 793.)

Dr. Emmons, who labored hard to reconcile this doctrine with the justice of God, would probably have been shocked at this candid admission of Dr. Schaff; but the strenuous efforts he made to strengthen this obviously weak point in his theological system only shows that he was aware of one of its greatest difficulties. Indeed, there is seldom a writer on this doctrine who does not, consciously or unconsciously, betray its essential defect.

SAD AND LAMENTABLE.

We know, for instance, of no preacher, on the subject of the few that are saved, who more implicitly believed it than Henry Scougal of Aberdeen, 1650–1678. He

even praised the curiosity of the man who asked Jesus
the question recorded in Luke; but the "sad and lamentable" side of the doctrine did not escape his notice. In
his sermon entitled "That there are but a Small Number
Saved," he says: —

" Seeing we are assured that there are different and very opposite estates of departed souls, some being admitted into happiness,
and others doomed to misery, beyond anything that we can conceive; this may put them upon farther inquiry, how mankind
is like to be divided ? Whether heaven or hell shall have the
greater share ? Such a laudable curiosity as this it was, that
put one of our blessed Saviour's followers to propose the question
in the text: 'Lord, are there few that be saved?'" (Scougal,
Works, p. 131.)

"Duty doth oblige us, and the Holy Scriptures will warrant
us to assure you, that there are very few that shall be saved;
that the whole world lieth in wickedness; and that they are a
little flock to whom the Father will give the kingdom." (Ib.,
p. 134.)

" The doctrine we have been insisting on is sad and lamentable; but the consideration of it may be very useful. It must
needs touch any serious person with a great deal of grief and
trouble to behold a multitude of people convened together, and to
think that, before thirty or forty years, a little more or great
deal less, they shall all go down unto the dark and silent grave,
and the greater, the far greater, part of their souls shall be
damned unto endless and unspeakable torments." (Ib., p. 147.)

The conflict of the moral sense with the supposed facts
of revelation is apparent in the following: —

" When we have said all that we can say, there are many that
will never be persuaded of the truth of that which we have been
proving. They cannot think it consistent with the goodness and
mercy of God, that the greatest part of mankind should be
damned; they cannot imagine that heaven should be such an
empty and desolate place, and have so very few to inhabit it.
But oh, what folly and madness is this, for sinful men to set
rules unto the divine goodness, and draw conclusions from it so
expressly contrary to what himself hath revealed!" (Ib.,
p. 146.)

There are still many who think it "folly and madness" to dispute Orthodox interpretations of the Scripture, or the theological tenets concerning the destiny of man which have been founded upon them; but the moral sense can no longer be defrauded of its right to "prove all things, and hold fast that which is good;" and we may feel perfectly confident that declarations or interpretations of Scripture, affirmations or anathemas of creeds, and all practical or theoretical assumptions concerning God and humanity which affront the moral sense, must sooner or later be abandoned.

EXCRUCIATING THOUGHTS.

In a missionary sermon delivered in 1834, Rev. Gardiner Spring, D.D., of New York, presented with great power some of the "excruciating thoughts" which believers in this doctrine must inevitably suffer: —

"Who can tell if some poor Pagan is not this day struggling for the assurance of a happy immortality, who 'through your mercy might have obtained mercy.' To the hopes of the dying believer he is a stranger. He never dwelt in a Christian land. He never heard a sermon, nor saw a Bible. He knows not that the blood of Jesus cleanseth from all sin. No; he is the victim of a dark and dreadful idolatry! Around his bed of death gather the shades of an impenetrable night. Over his prospects for eternity are collected heavy and dense clouds of unappeased indignation. Approach and see. His bosom is torn and distracted with anguish. His lips quiver with agony, and he draws his last gasp in despair! And oh, that it were one solitary Pagan only! But, think of *twenty-five millions* of your fellow-men every year sinking in such a death; and then look into that deep abyss, where millions after millions of years roll on, and the miserable sufferers encounter new dangers, new fears, new scenes of anguish, without any prospect of termination; and what emotions of grief, abasement, and horror may smite our bosoms! 'We are verily guilty concerning our brother.' Here are miseries which our faithfulness might have relieved. But for our guilty slumber, multitudes of these immortal beings might have been trained to a happy immortality. *Excruciating thought!* O immeasurable responsibility! because the remedy for these woes is in our hands. Sin infinite! to be washed away only by atoning blood." (pp. 28, 29.)

DARK AND DISTRESSING.

Rev. Samuel Miller, D.D., Professor in the Theological Seminary, Princeton, N. J., thus calculated in 1835: —

" Of the eight hundred millions of the world's population, but little more than an *eightieth* part are even professors of religion in any Scriptural form, or claim to know anything of its sanctifying power. . . . Such is, confessedly, at present the *dark and distressing* state of the great mass of our world's population. . . . What a little remnant, among all the multiplied millions of mankind, have any adequate or *saving* knowledge of the religion of Christ!" (*Sermon before the American Board,* 1835, p. 15.)

AN AWFUL VIEW.

The following, from a sermon before the American Board in 1859, by Rev. Robert W. Patterson, D.D., of Chicago, completely concedes the two points we have endeavored to establish; namely, that the "majority" are doomed to endless woe by Orthodoxy; and secondly, that the doctrine is one "awful" to contemplate. It is urged by Dr. Patterson as a motive for missionary effort: —

" The great Scriptural doctrine that this is the only place of probation to the members of our fallen race, and that those who die out of Christ are lost forever, sets *before our minds an awful view of the destiny that awaits the majority of the living generation of our race;* while it presses home an appeal to the sympathies of all who know the value and preciousness of the Christian hope, which must, if anything can, stir them up to *make haste* and send the word of life to their dying fellow-sinners. It bids us to keep in mind that the *time is short* within which there can be anything done to save the six hundred millions of heathen, and the three or four millions of Mohammedans and dead formalists and heartless unbelievers, who are now hastening to

the close of their probationary life without any preparation for
a happy eternity.   And it admonishes us to remember that we
ourselves can have, at the most, only a few years to be spent in
efforts to rescue the souls of our fellow-heirs of immortality
from the woes of the second death." (p. 34.)

PERSONAL EXPERIENCE.

It may not be wholly out of place for the writer to add
his own experience. With humiliation, and with all charity
for those from whom he now differs, he must confess that
he once held this doctrine himself. He was taught, on
uniting with the Christian Church, that it was infallibly
revealed in the Scriptures. He recalls the sense of hum-
ble gratitude he experienced when he felt that God had
called him from before the foundation of the world to
be an heir of glory, while millions of others better entitled
to this distinction, the vast majority of the race, were left
to perish. He recalls, too, the terrible conflict which this
conviction had to encounter with his sentiments of justice
and benevolence; his struggle with creeds, texts, and
"divine decrees," until finally he determined to "let God
be true, though every man a liar."

2. Evangelical Protests.

The admissions we have presented, conceding — with
dark, mysterious, sad, lamentable, awful, and various other
adjectives — the painful and difficult features of this view
of the eternal destiny of the vast majority of the race,
have been taken entirely from Evangelical writers, most
of them accepting the doctrine and seeing no way of
escape from it. We now call to the witness-stand another
class of Evangelical writers, — those who have felt the
difficulties and implications of this dogma so strongly
that they have been obliged to abandon some of its most
obnoxious features and to protest against them. Most of
these protests are not directed against the assumption of

the eternal *doom* of the majority, but against the assumption that it is the *majority* of mankind that are
eternally doomed. It is the first assumption that constitutes the chief horror of this doctrine. If that were
removed, there would be no need to protest against the
second. Arminians have generally been quite as guilty
as Calvinists in teaching the endless misery of those who
are damned; but the battle between them has related
mainly to the extent of the atonement, the conditions
of salvation, and the proportion of those who should avail
themselves of it. As we have seen in the chapter on
the Evangelical Creeds, the Arminians bitterly reproached
the Calvinists for teaching the damnation of the majority
of mankind. Calvinism has never been able to clear its
skirts of this reproach. It is a natural and logical inference from its theological system; it is indelibly written
in its creeds and inscribed in its literature, and remains
to-day, as we have shown, an acknowledged tenet of its
modern advocates. Arminianism, on the other hand, —
while in some of its presentations it has taken refuge in
the miserable device of water baptism to wash out from
the blood of infants the taint of inherited sin, — has refused
either to damn infants on account of Adam's transgression, or to damn the heathen for not accepting a gospel
which had never been presented to them. In its rejection
of the harsh, high Calvinistic views of predestination and
reprobation, in its proclamation of an unlimited atonement and the freedom of all men to accept it, Arminianism did much to relieve our conception of the character
of God from the imputation which these doctrines have
cast upon it.

NOT JESUS BUT THE DEVIL.

The reproaches which modern Universalists and Unitarians have cast upon Orthodoxy, for teaching the damnation of the majority, have not been more severe than those

which have sometimes been hurled at it from Evangelical
and Anti-Calvinistic sources.   Curio, in 1569, instead of
attributing the opinion of the fewness of the saved to
Jesus, went so far as to attribute it to the devil, arguing
that God wished to pour forth his goodness and pity on
the most, and not on the few.[1]   Curio was much abused
for the book, but two hundred years later Charles Wesley
made precisely the same charge.   Those who have known
the Methodist poet only in his milder devotional hymns
may be surprised to see with what bitter sarcasm, pointed
invective, and intense feeling he opposed the Calvinistic
assumption of the doom of the majority.   His series of
hymns entitled " Hymns on God's Everlasting Love " are
nearly all of them directed against what he calls this
" hellish blasphemy."   Note the keen irony and bold
denunciation of the following : —

CHARLES WESLEY'S PROTEST.

" Ah! gentle gracious Dove,
    And art Thou griev'd in me,
That sinners should restrain thy love,
    And say, ' It is not free;
    It is not free for *all*:
    The *most* Thou passest by,
And mockest with a fruitless call
    Whom Thou hast doom'd to die.'

" They think Thee not sincere
    In giving each his day,
Thou only draw'st the sinner near,
    To cast him quite away :
    To aggravate his Sin,
    His sure damnation seal:
Thou shew'st him heaven, and say'st, ' Go in,'
    And thrust'st him into hell.

[1] Quoted by Farrar, "Mercy and Judgment," p. 25.

" O Horrible Decree,[1]
Worthy of whence it came!
Forgive their hellish blasphemy,
   Who charge it on the Lamb:
Whose pity Him inclin'd
To leave his throne above,
The friend and Saviour of mankind,
The God of grace and love.

.   .   .   .   .

" To limit Thee they dare,
Blaspheme Thee to thy face,
Deny their fellow-worms a share
In thy redeeming grace:
All for their own they take,
Thy righteousness engross,
Of none effect to *most* they make
The merits of thy cross.

"Sinners, abhor the fiend,
His other gospel hear,
The God of truth did not intend
The thing His words declare;
He offers grace to all,
Which *most* cannot embrace,
Mock'd with an ineffectual call,
And insufficient grace.

" The righteous God consign'd
Them over to their doom,
And sent the Saviour of mankind
To damn them from the womb;
To damn for falling short
Of what they could not do,
For not believing the report
Of that which was not true.

---

[1] Whenever Wesley uses these words in these hymns he prints them in small capitals. The capitalization of pronouns referring to Deity is irregular.

6

"The God of Love past by
The most of those that fell,
Ordain'd poor reprobates to die,
　And forc'd them into hell,
　He did not do the deed,
　(Some have more mildly rav'd),
He did not damn them — but decreed
　They never should be sav'd.　　　　•

"He did not them bereave
　Of Life, or stop their breath,
His grace he only would not give,
　And starv'd their souls to death.
　Satanic sophistry!
　But still all-gracious God,
They charge the sinner's death on Thee,
　Who bought'st him with thy blood.

"They think with shrieks and cries
　To please the Lord of Hosts,
And offer Thee, in sacrifice,
　Millions of slaughter'd ghosts;
　With new-born babes they fill
　The dire infernal shade,
For such (they say) was thy great will
　Before the world was made.

"How long, O God, how long
　Shall *Satan's* rage proceed!
Wilt Thou not soon avenge the wrong,
　And crush the serpent's head!
　Surely Thou shalt at last
　Bruise him beneath our feet;
The devil, and his doctrine cast
　Into the burning pit.

"Arise, O God, arise,
　Thy glorious truth maintain,
Hold forth the bloody sacrifice
　For every sinner slain!

Defend thy mercy's cause,
Thy grace divinely free ;
Lift up the standard of thy cross,
Draw all men unto thee."

(*Hymns on God's Everlasting Love*, Hymn XVII. p. 30.)

In another hymn Wesley indignantly disclaims "the devil's doctrine :" —

"God forbid, that I should dare
To charge my death on Thee:
No, thy truth and mercy tear
The HORRIBLE DECREE!
Tho' the devil's doom I meet,
The devil's doctrine I disclaim;
Let it sink into the pit
Of hell, from whence it came.

(Hymn VII. p. 14.)

The following is Wesley's not very courteous explanation of Calvinism : —

" They would not the pure truth receive,
.   Sav'd when they might, they would not be,
God therefore left them to believe
The devil's HORRIBLE DECREE:
And lo! they still believe a lye,
That God did *Nine in Ten* pass by.

" In them the strong delusion reigns,
That none but they in CHRIST have hope,
The poison spreads throughout their veins,
And drinks their angry spirits up ;
' Let all but us in *Tophet* dwell,
Away with reprobates to hell.' "

(Hymn X. p. 62.)

In the following he thanks God for restraining him from believing in "the devil's law :" —

> "I could the devil's law receive,
>   Unless restrain'd by thee;
> I could, (good God!) I could believe
>   The HORRIBLE DECREE.

> "I could believe that God is Hate,
>   The God of love and grace
> Did damn, pass by, *and reprobate*
>   *The most of human race.*

> "Farther than this I cannot go,
>   Till *Tophet* take me in:
> But O forbid that I should know
>   This mystery of sin."
>   (Hymn VI. p. 52.)

Wesley even prays that his hate of this doctrine may be increased; but the reader of these poems will be inclined to agree with his surmise that that is hardly possible : —

> "Increase (if that can be)
>   The perfect hate I feel
> To Satan's HORRIBLE DECREE,
>   That genuine child of hell ;
> Which feigns Thee to *pass by*
>   *The most of Adam's race,*
> And leave them in their blood to die,
>   Shut out from saving grace."
>   (Hymn XII. p. 66.)

MODERN METHODIST PROTEST.

Methodism has maintained this attitude towards Calvinism down to the present day. But a few weeks since, Rev. W. F. Mallalieu, D.D., of Boston, said, in *Zion's Herald* (Jan. 31, 1883), the Methodist paper of that city : —

"The fact must pretty soon become apparent that Orthodoxy will have to give up Calvinism, with all its narrowness and incongruity, or it will disintegrate at a rate so rapid that living men will see the last of it. It is too late in the history of the world to undertake to defend the dogmas of Calvinism; they deserve neither defence nor apology; they have dishonored God and his gospel from the very first; they have been an immeasurable hindrance to the triumphs of Christianity; and the sooner they are buried in the grave of oblivion, the better for all concerned."

The *Central Christian Advocate*, an organ of the Methodist Church, published at St. Louis, said in its issue of Feb. 28, 1883 : —

" Now the humanity and spirituality of this century has thoroughly undermined the principles of this un-Christian theology. Men are no longer willing to believe that immortal souls are consigned to eternal punishment without having a chance of salvation. And this doctrine of a probation after death is simply a metaphysical scheme to save a tottering theological system. . . . Methodism has taught, and will continue to teach, that Christ died for all men, and that all men will be saved who make the best of the light, talents, and opportunities which God offers them. We do not claim to be able to explain the divine methods perfectly, but we affirm with confidence that God is the loving Father, wise, just, merciful, and loving, not desiring the death of any, but offering them spiritual help and salvation. Probation after death is simply a speculation, and does not commend itself to thoughtful men. Christ teaches us plainly how to meet these questions to which there is no definite answer in his own words. When one came unto him and asked, ' Are they few that be saved ? ' his answer was, ' Strive to enter in at the strait gate ; for many, I say unto you, will seek to enter in, and shall not be able.' "

Though the Methodist Church has taken strong ground against the doom of the *majority*, and though the doctrine of everlasting punishment is not taught in its " Twenty-five Articles of Religion " drawn up by John Wesley, yet Methodists, in common with other Arminian bodies, have preached the *endless doom* of the minority. The fear of hell has been a great weapon in Methodist revivals, and

the future destiny of all those who reject the atonement
of Christ has been described in lurid, sulphurous language.
There is no worse description of the horrors of hell in
Jonathan Edwards, Boston, or Wigglesworth, than may
be found in Charles Wesley's hymn entitled "The Cry of
a Reprobate."[1]

EPISCOPALIAN PROTESTS.

Some of the most earnest and determined opponents of
this doctrine of the doom of the majority have been found
among preachers and writers of the Church of England.
We need only refer to a few.

A striking repudiation of the doctrine is found in a tract
entitled "God's Sovereignty and his Universal Love to
the Souls of Men reconciled, in a reply to Mr. Jonathan
Dickinson," by John Beach, A.M., Boston, 1747; and a
second tract by the same author entitled "A Second Vindication of God's Sovereign Free Grace indeed," Boston,
1748. In the course of this debate Mr. Beach said: —

"But to draw the Picture of the ever-blessed God according
to our Idea of the very worst of Beings ; to represent him as an
Hater of *the greater Part of Mankind*, as one who hated his own
Offspring before they were born, and resolved to damn them to
Hell-Torments before they had done Good or Evil, or were capable of offending him, merely to shew his Sovereignty, and that
he can do what he pleases with his own; as one whose Justice is
such, that he sets the Children's Teeth on Edge, because their
Father had eaten sour Grapes Thousands of Years before they
were born; and makes them a motly Mixture of *Beast and Devil*,
as fast as he gives them Being, because Adam sinned, which
was not in their Power to prevent, as one whose Love to the
Souls of men is so very little that when all might have been
redeemed by Christ's Passion as well as a few, he of his meer
Pleasure chose *that the bigger Part by far of them who equally
needed it*, and would have equally improved it, should be excluded,
and shut out, and have no Part or Share in it; not because it

[1] Hymns on God's Everlasting Love ; Hymn XI. p. 21.

would have made any Addition to Christ's Sufferings, but merely because God did not chuse that they should be saved. And though he declares his most tender Love to Mankind, and his compassionate Concern for their Salvation, and intreats them to be happy, and swears to them that he does not will their Death, but their Conversion and Life, and asks them affectionately, why they will die? and how long it will be ere they be made clean? and what could be done for them more? and wishes they would hearken to him, and says: O that thou hadst known the Things that belong to thy Peace, yet notwithstanding all this Show of Mercy, his secret Decree and unchangeable Will and Desire is, that the most of them shall burn forever in that Fire prepared for the obstinate Devil and his Angels. And therefore would not that his Son should effectually redeem them, or his Spirit yield them sufficient Grace, without which he knew, they could no more escape Hell than they could shun Death. Now when we represent God to our Minds surrounded with this amazing Horror, how can we prevent our Hearts rising against him, and wishing there was no such God. I profess for my Part, I had rather a Million Times, never to have had a Being, than to think thus of God." (*A Second Vindication of God's Sovereign Free Grace indeed*, p. 80.)

More than a hundred years have passed since this was written, and, sad to relate, there is still occasion for the same protest.

Mr. Beach further said in regard to the heathen: —

" You take it for granted, that we have the same Notion of the Heathen World, as you have of the Reprobates who were doomed to Hell-Fire before they were born, and when brought into Being are left under a Necessity of being wicked and miserable; but you are very much mistaken; for we utterly deny that the Heathen are left under a Necessity of being Eternally miserable, and I am sure you cannot prove it till the day of Judgment, when we shall see how God will deal with them." (*God's Sovereignty and His Universal Love, &c.*, p. 38.)

Dr. Thomas Pyle, Canon of Sarum, and author of " A Paraphrase on the Acts of the Apostles and the

Epistles," devotes two of his Sixty Sermons to the theme,
" Are there few that be saved ?" and says : —

" Honest and well-meaning Christians, whose lot in life hap-
pens to fall in an age of irreligion and vice, are wont to be
disheartened at the woful prospect of the final state of their
fellow-creatures. To think that the far greater part of their own
species, of their own *image*, will utterly perish and be undone,
is a most *uncomfortable* thought." (*Pyle's Sermons*, 1773,
p. 438.)

" From a right interpretation of these Scriptures, must appear
the strange and wretched mistake of those Christians who
ascribe the smallness of the number of such as they *suppose* will
be saved, to some absolute and arbitrary decree of God, by
which he selects a chosen few, and rejects all others, — an opinion
against which men can never be too often cautioned ; since it
effaces, and strikes out, every amiable character that is given us
of God, and spoils the whole sense and purpose of our gospel
account of rewards and punishments." (*Ibid.*, p. 442.)

" These Scriptures never make, nor were ever designed to
make, any absolute comparison between the *numbers* of such as
will be finally saved, or finally lost. They only set forth the
qualifications requisite to save *all* men; namely, righteousness,
and a watchful care, and a good improvement of the talents and
graces committed to us all ; and the certain reasons why *any*
will be left to perish, viz., wilful negligence, and deliberate
vice." (*Ibid.*, p. 428.)

Bishop Colenso of Natal, after quoting passages from
an American Missionary Report, in which the heathen are
sorrowfully consigned to hell (see page 66, *ante*), enters
" a solemn protest against such views, as utterly contrary
to the whole spirit of the Gospel, — as obscuring the Grace
of God and perverting his message of Love and Good-
will to Man, and operating with most injurious and dead-
ening effect, both on those who teach and on those who
are taught." [1]

[1] Ten Weeks in Natal, p. 253.

Rev. F. Nutcombe Oxenham, in his reply to Dr. Pusey already referred to, entitled, "What is the Truth as to Everlasting Punishment," shows that the doctrine that the vast majority are to be lost has contributed very largely to undermine belief in endless punishment. This is one of the few things for which we have to thank this painful dogma: —

"No doubt it is perfectly true, as Dr. Pusey intimates, that the thought of these vast multitudes ' going away ' to suffer the ' damnum ' which awaits all evil-doers, has contributed very largely to enforce a conviction that this ' damnum,' this punishment, will not be endless. It has done so, and it ought to have done so, and it always will do so; and as long as reasonable Christian men, not driven by the exigencies of controversy to rely on idle and groundless sophistries, form their belief in this matter not simply, though primarily, on the testimony of Holy Scriptures, but also on the teaching of what they see in the world around them, they will continue to believe that ' the wicked,' those who die wicked, are many and not few, a *vast multitude*, — fearful to contemplate, whether they are actually a numerical majority of all mankind or not; and they will not believe that all these are hopelessly and finally lost, that all these will be kept alive forever, simply to be ' punished with the devil.' " (p. 42.)

Canon Farrar we may expect to find warmly denouncing the popular views: —

" If the popular views be true, the multiplication of the human race is an unmitigated evil,·for it serves mainly to people with agonizing myriads an endless hell. If the popular views be true — if most souls are lost — then to bring human beings into the world can be little 'short of a selfish crime." (*Mercy and Judgment*, p. 138.)

Canon Farrar has not stated his protest any too strongly.

CONGREGATIONAL PROTESTS.

There have not been wanting Congregational ministers also who have disowned and rebuked this doctrine, though they have been obliged to deny Calvinism and oppose

Congregational confessions of faith in order to do so.
Rev. W. W. Patton, in an article on the True Theory of
Missions, quotes the tenth chapter of the Westminster
Confession,[1] which plumply consigns the whole heathen
world to eternal destruction, and says : —

" This is sufficiently positive, especially as it contradicts both
our Saviour and the Apostle Paul. It represents heathen who
live according to their light as ' much less ' able to be saved than
men who hear the gospel and reject it, thus directly contradicting
our Saviour, who declared that those who rejected his words
would receive a heavier condemnation than even the depraved,
unrepentant inhabitants of Sodom and Gomorrah, or Tyre and
Sidon (Matt. xi. 20–24).   The ' Confession of Faith ' declares
the salvation of conscientious heathen to be ' much less ' possible than that of unbelieving hearers of the gospel; while Christ
asserts, that even the most flagrant sinners of the heathen shall
find it ' more tolerable ' in the day of Judgment, than such
unbelievers.   Equally at variance with the ' Confession of
Faith ' is the declaration of Paul in Rom. ii. 14, 26, 27, in which
he shows how those ' having not the law may be a law unto
themselves,' and how their ' uncircumcision shall be counted for
circumcision.' "   (Bibliotheca Sacra, July, 1858, p. 553.)

Dr. Patton exposes the moral objections to this doctrine
with considerable force : —

" It is revolting to our moral sense. . . . To assert gravely,
then, that the heathen who have never heard of Christ, are shut
out from all possible hope of pardon and are not in a salvable
position in their present circumstances, is to offend the moral
sense of thoughtful men, as well as that, of the common multitude. . . . Such a theory practically denies the divine grace by
suspending its exercise, so far as the heathen (the majority of the
human race) are concerned, upon the action of those already
enlightened.   It declares that there is no possible mercy for the
heathen unless Christians choose to carry the gospel to them.
Does it seem rational, or in harmony with the universality and
freedom of God's grace, that the only possibility of salvation

[1] Quoted on p. 41.

for the mass of mankind should be suspended, not on anything within their control, but on the conduct of men on the opposite side of the globe? By such representations the minds of men are shocked, and a reaction takes place, which is unfavorable not only to the cause of missions, but to evangelical religion as well." (*Ibid.*, p. 554.)

Rev. Washington Gladden, in a discourse printed in the Springfield *Republican*, March 15, 1879, after making various citations showing the harsh nature of Calvinism, said : —

" Do not the citations that I have shown you, outlining the history of several doctrines, indicate that the men who framed and taught these doctrines must have been somewhat deficient in moral perception? Could their ideas of right and wrong have been very clear? I bring against them no railing accusation. Out of their own mouths you have been permitted to judge them. I believe that most of them were good men, that many of them were brave, faithful, self-sacrificing, that we may find in their conduct worthy examples of purity and consecration; but I do not think that their moral standards, their notions of justice and righteousness, can be accepted at this day."

OTHER PROTESTS.

The Boston *Sunday Herald* (Jan. 7, 1883), in an article entitled " Hell-Fire Missions," says : —

" The doom of the majority is one of those theological fictions which can be traced to a strictly human origin, and is against the belief in a whole God, a whole Christ, and a true realization of the ends of human existence."

The New York *Independent*, Jan. 16, 1883, admits that some way out of this doctrine must be found. In discussing the question of probation after death, it says : —

" Only one thing will persuade thinking men to adopt it ; and that will be the conviction that, without it, God's experiment of humanity is a failure, and that there are few that be saved. If it be really true that on this theory the great majority of the world are lost, if that be the outcome of the New England theology, as the *Christian Register* is now trying to show in reply to Dr. Withrow, then we may be sure that some escape from that conclusion will be sought, if not by adopting Dorner's theory, then by some improvement on the New England theology. We confess that we are startled by what Mr. Cook [1] yields as to the salvation of the heathen. He says, ' Human nature is such, however, that only a few among millions do accept the essential Christ of conscience.' We do not see how that can be safely asserted.''

PRACTICAL FAILURE OF THE DOCTRINE.

In addition to the admissions and testimonies we have presented to the moral and theoretical difficulties of the doctrine, a powerful argument against it is found in its inadequacy as a practical missionary motive. We have shown in the previous chapter how constantly the lost state of the vast majority of mankind has been urged as an incentive to missionary zeal. It has failed, however, to convert the heathen world, because the heathen cannot be made to realize their eternally lost condition. We acknowledge the great good foreign missions have accomplished; but what they have wrought for the elevation, instruction, and improvement of the temporal condition of the heathen, whatever they have done towards ushering in a nobler form of life, cannot be credited to the preaching of this doctrine. These incidental and practical results are to us the really valuable features of missionary work; but they are not what has been primarily aimed at, and they could more easily have been achieved by more direct means. We have the confession of Dr. Hopkins, Dr. Goodwin, and a host of preachers, that all these results are inadequate compared with the salvation of the heathen soul. Nevertheless, after all that has been done, the heathen are not converted; the vast majority, if Orthodoxy

[1] For Mr. Joseph Cook's attempted palliation of the doctrine, see paragraph on " The Essential Christ " in the succeeding chapter."

be true, are still under this terrible curse, and daily going to a horrible doom. In a missionary sermon delivered in 1863, Rev. Dr. Cleaveland, of New Haven, said:—

"Fifty years ago the heathen were estimated, in round numbers, at six hundred millions. You remember how those terrific figures, emblazoned before the eyes of Christendom, trumpeted in startling appeals from land to land, were employed by the Holy Ghost as one of the grand arguments that first roused the Church to the work of modern missions. Now let me ask, What, after a half-century of missionary labor, is the present number of the heathen? Can we report any material diminution in those dreadful figures? Can we reduce them by so much as one million, or even half a million? No. Thousands and tens of thousands have been brought to Christ, but there are six hundred millions still! The banner of the cross has been planted in almost every pagan land, and many are the witnesses for Jesus among those idolaters. Still there are the countless masses of India, the untrodden depths of Africa, and the unexplored regions of China ; as if, in defiance of all our efforts, heathenism still glories in her proud temples, still whitens the earth with the bones of her victims, and darkens the sky with the smoke of her idolatrous sacrifices. . . . Glorious things have been achieved, it is true. But, after all, there are the six hundred millions still groping in the shadow of death, and *perishing, twenty millions a year!*"

We have already noted the confession of Rev. Dr. Kirk, "that more pagans are born, more die, in one year, than have been converted in over fifty years."

But this motive has not only proved inadequate to convert the heathen ; it has also failed to impress Christians with its truthfulness. The Christian world has never acted as if it really believed this terrible doctrine. Now and then, under the influence of missionary meetings, when the lost state of the heathen has been presented as a motive with earnestness and power, spasmodic efforts have been made to conceive and act upon it as if it were a dreadful reality; but such results have only been temporary. The Orthodox Christian world lives, for the most part, as if the doctrine were not true. The missionaries themselves have again and again arraigned the indifference of Christians on this subject so thoroughly as to relieve us from the necessity of any such disagreeable task. Rev. George H. Pond, a Presbyterian missionary, shows how fully this idea has taken hold upon the churches : —

" They often hear the Macedonian cry come up from the perishing millions, and they echo that cry in the ears of the churches at home, and still there is no response, or, if the churches return an answer, it is often only that the treasuries are empty, or that the men cannot be found who are willing to go ; while it is well known that multitudes in these very churches are amassing wealth by hundreds, by thousands, and by tens of thousands, and that scores and hundreds of ministers even are seeking in vain to crowd themselves into the towns and cities of our own country, many of which are already more than supplied. Does not this state of things evince an astonishing amount of unbelief on the part of multitudes of the professed friends of Jesus and 'of his cause on earth? . If not, what does it mean, when we see countless multitudes of our fellow-creatures groping their dark way down to the regions of death and hell, perishing for lack of knowledge, with no one to instruct them, while our churches are full of the professed followers of the toiling, suffering, self-sacrificing Saviour, who are loading, burdening, themselves with costly but useless and often disgusting ornaments to feed their vanity, and luxuriating in wealth while their Lord's treasury is empty, or only stingily supplied with a very small part of the unused surplus of the proud rich, mingled with the mites of the poor. . . .

" The *churches do not believe the testimony of Scriptures* touching this matter. They do not believe that the heathen will be turned into hell with all the nations that forget God. . . . They do not believe that the gospel can renovate and save the degraded and idolatrous nations, and that ' there is no other name,' except the name of Jesus, ' given under heaven, whereby we must be saved.' " (*Presbyterian Quarterly Review*, Jan. 1861.)

Such an arraignment of the Church from a Christian missionary is very significant. It shows what has always been apparent, that the professed belief of Christians and their actual belief on this subject are wider apart than the gulf which separated Dives from Lazarus.

Bishop Colenso, himself a missionary to the heathen, rejecting this doctrine of the damnation of the heathen, thus reproaches those who profess to believe it: —

" Why! if such be indeed the condition of the heathen world, how can a Christian comfortably eat butter with his bread, ride in a carriage, wear a fine nap upon his coat, or enjoy one of the commonest blessings of daily life? What a monster of selfishness that man must be, who could endure the thought of ease, or enjoyment in body or soul, for himself, while such was the horrible destiny of so many millions of his fellow-men, simply because they knew not — had never heard of — that name of Love, and the Hope of Life Eternal." (*Ten Weeks in Natal*, p. 253.)

V.

ATTEMPTED MITIGATIONS.

THE preceding chapter has made it evident that there are many who are not insensible to the intellectual and ethical difficulties of this doctrine. With Dr. Barnes, Dr. Shedd, and Dr. Schaff, they admit the " dark and awful " character of a belief which consigns millions on millions of mankind to endless woe; but accepting without question the premises on which the doctrine is founded, they see no way to avoid the logic of the doctrine itself. They therefore take refuge in an entrenchment to which Calvinism has often been obliged to retreat when hotly pressed by its opponents; they hide themselves in the very darkness they have created, saying, with Dr. Schaff, it is " a deep and dark mystery; " or, with Dr. Albert Barnes, " It is all dark, dark to my soul, and I cannot disguise it."

There are no manifestations of the strength of the religious sentiment which are more sublime than when it throws itself back upon its trust in the mercy and goodness of God, though it can see no intellectual or moral ground for affirming them. Such occasions may arise in individual experiences in practical life, when the view of God's dealings is limited to single and isolated examples, or confined to a small portion of time; they do not arise, however, in any large and enlightened conception of God and of the universe which he governs. To take, as Calvinism asks us to do, a sweeping view of the whole universe, over immeasurable eternities, embracing the entire history of God's dealings with the whole human race, — not only here, but in the interminable future in which human destiny is conceived to be fixed, — and then to admit that our conception of God is one which cannot be reconciled with his mercy and goodness, is to put the religious sentiment to a greater strain than it can be expected to bear. However admirable the strength this sentiment has exhibited in coping with this difficulty, we deem it a far higher and purer exhibition of its authority, when, instead of meekly acknowledging such conceptions of the dark nature of God and of his government, it grandly refuses to accept the premises on which they are founded.

To admit that God has so created and governed the world that the vast majority of the race are destined to perish, is a reflection upon the divine mercy and goodness; but also upon the divine wisdom. A farmer who, by his own inaction, should allow the greatest portion of his crop to rot when he might have gathered it all, would be considered a poor farmer. A king who should so manage his realm as to involve the far greater part of his subjects in hopeless misery, would be considered a very unskilful ruler. If we knew, also, that it was in his power, by a simple royal mandate, to grant to every one of his subjects the happiness enjoyed by a few, we should think

he had a bad heart if he did not issue it. It is no wonder, then, that Calvinism has often writhed under the
reproaches which have been cast upon it for teaching the
damnation of the majority, and that it has sought in
various ways to soften the harshness of the doctrine.
These earnest attempts show the modifications which
have taken place in Calvinism itself. It has widely
departed from its historic and original form. The current Calvinism of the day is at variance with its ancient
standards. We have already referred to the change of
view which has taken place in regard to infant damnation.
Early Calvinism asserted it; modern Calvinism repudiates
it, though it still holds to creeds which naturally imply it.
These departures from early Calvinism are the result of
the pressure of a nobler view of Christianity, and the
development of a higher form of civilization. As Channing well said : " Calvinism has to contend with foes more
formidable than theologians ; with foes from whom it
cannot shield itself in mystery and metaphysical subtili-
ties — we mean with the progress of the human mind,
and with the progress of the spirit of the gospel." [1]

The expedients which have been invented to save Calvinism have acted powerfully to disintegrate it. The
original system was mercilessly logical. Having laid
down his foundation premises, Calvin had the courage to
build his system upon them. He drew a straight line from
premise to conclusion. Modern Calvinism pretends to
accept the premises, but seeks to avoid the conclusions.
The line it draws is not straight, but sinuous. It falters,
wavers, and evades. The beautiful logical symmetry of
the system is destroyed. Modern Calvinism is inconsistent and contradictory. It seeks to read new meanings
into old documents. It invents explanations, probabilities,
and mitigations. Much of the strength of modern Calvinism is exerted in apologizing for its parentage, or in

[1] Moral Argument against Calvinism, p. 468.

the more fruitless task of trying to build a sightly and hospitable structure on the old foundation. Nevertheless, though inconsistent, illogical, and inartistic, there is more heart in the derived form than there was in the original. Early high Calvinism had looked so steadily at the face of its terrible Gorgon-God that, like those who gazed upon Medusa, it had well-nigh been turned into stone. But that Gorgonian head has lost much of its power to petrify human sensibility. There is a new leaven working to-day; and may we not hope that eventually the new leaven may purge out that which is old?

What now are some of the methods with which modern Orthodoxy seeks to avoid the reproach of this doctrine that the majority are lost?

THE INFANTILE QUIBBLE.

It is argued by some that as Protestants, both Calvinists and Arminians, now generally admit that all dying in infancy are saved, therefore, as the majority of the race die young, the majority of the race will be saved. This position is taken in defiance of the Westminster and the Augsburg confessions, both of which, historically interpreted, teach the damnation of infants. The numerical quibble affords no relief, however, from the moral difficulties of the doctrine; for it still remains true, according to Orthodoxy, that the vast majority of the adult portion of mankind are lost.

We are quite content to let our indictment of Calvinistic Orthodoxy rest upon the doctrines which it still teaches; we do not upbraid it for those it has outgrown. It still teaches that the vast majority of the adult population of the globe are doomed to irretrievable misery. It is this doctrine that we urge it to repudiate as blasphemous and untrue.

Canon Farrar was met with this quibble. He says:[1]—

[1] Mercy and Judgment, p. 140.

" Even in some of the so-called answers to my sermons, the difficulty was only met by the argument that ' the majority of mankind die in infancy and therefore that the majority of mankind would be saved.' It is not worth while to argue with writers who take refuge in quibbles. By the ' majority of mankind,' I mean, as all serious writers have meant, the majority of those who have attained to years of discretion. But by using such an argument these writers imply their belief, and it is still the common opinion of those who claim to be ' orthodox,' — too often at the expense of ' speaking deceitfully for God,' — that most men ' perish ; ' and by this they mean that most men pass after death 'into a life of endless torments.' They have not only held this, but further, — that the vast majority of Christians also pass after death into endless torments." (*Mercy and Judgment*, p. 140.)

THE MILLENNIAL HOPE.

Another attempted mitigation is the millennial hope. This has been a source of consolation to many. It is the faith that ultimately the whole world will be converted ; and, when all are gathered in, " the number of the lost will be inconsiderable as compared with the whole number of the saved."

Thus the late Dr. Charles Hodge says, in his Commentary on Romans v. 20 : —

" Since the half of mankind die in infancy, and, according to the Protestant doctrine, are heirs of salvation ; and since, in the future state of the Church, the knowledge of the Lord is to cover the earth, — we have reason to believe that the lost shall bear to the saved no greater proportion than the inmates of a prison do to the mass of the community."

Rev. Albert Barnes, whose pathetic admission we have published in a preceding chapter, found comfort in the same view, which may be found in his Commentary on Isaiah liii. 11 : —

" It is morally certain that a large portion of the race, taken as a whole, will enter into heaven. *Hitherto the number has been small. The great mass have rejected him and have been lost.* But there are brighter times before the church and the world. The pure gospel of the Redeemer is yet to spread around the globe, and it is yet to become, and to be for ages, the religion of the world. Age after age is to roll on when all shall know him and obey him; and in those future times, what immense multitudes shall enter into heaven. So that it may yet be seen, that the number of those who will be lost from the whole human family, compared with those who will be saved, will be no greater in proportion than the criminals in a well-organized community who are imprisoned are, compared with the number of obedient, virtuous, and peaceful citizens.''

This is the single ray of light on this subject that seemed to come to Dr. Barnes. It is a new evidence of the depth of the darkness which oppressed him, when he was forced to take comfort in this millennial device. In a recent article in the *Christian Intelligencer*,[1] Rev. William Rankin Duryee, D.D., presents this same hope. Rev. S. W. Boardman, D.D., in a letter to the writer, says: —

" It is *undoubtedly the opinion* of most Orthodox Christians that the *great majority of the human race, who have as yet died* in mature years, are lost, but their hope is that when the whole race shall have been brought into existence, and human history on earth be completed, the great majority of all will have been saved.''

It is to be noted, in the first place, that this is an individual opinion. It is not supported by the Church creeds; and those who, like Dr. Withrow, insist that their orthodoxy shall be interpreted only through the standards, cannot consistently appeal to it. Dr. Schaff says that this opinion — that the number of those who are ultimately lost is very inconsiderable as compared with the whole number of the saved — " would be preposterous in the Augustinian and Roman Catholic systems." We may add with confidence, that it would be equally preposterous in the Calvinistic system. The straits to which that system has been

[1] " Quantity in Salvation," Christian Intelligencer, Feb. 14, 1883.

driven by Arminianism are illustrated in this curious attempt to escape from one of the logical consequences of Calvinism.

But let us examine the implications of this millennial device, and see how much relief it really affords.

In the first place it concedes that, up to the present time at least, and until some remote future, the doctrine we arraign is true. This concession is not merely left to be inferred. Dr. Barnes and Dr. Boardman, with the score of authorities previously quoted, directly express it. "Hitherto," says Dr. Barnes, "the number has been small. The great mass have rejected him and been lost." The hope is entertained that at some future time the proportions may be reversed. This hope for the future does nothing to relieve the terrible blackness of the present and the past. It does not relieve the condition of the vast majority who have thus far been damned; it does not relieve of its blackness the character of the God who has been guilty of damning them. Though it alters the proportion, it does not lessen in any degree the absolute number of the lost. That number is still left so great as to be positively inconceivable. In his sermon before the American Board, Rev. Dr. Skinner, of the Presbyterian Church, calculated that the heathen had been passing to their eternal destiny, strangers to the influence of God's recovering grace, at the rate of 20,000,000 a year. 20,000,-000 a year is a small estimate of the number of those heathen who have died without accepting the gospel; but, even at this rate, the accumulation is frightful. 20,000,000, multiplied by 1882, gives a total of 37,640,000,-000 souls in hell since the beginning of the Christian era alone. Of the millions who were damned before it, Dr. Skinner makes no estimate. How long it will be before the whole world is converted we cannot tell; but, at the present slow rate of progress, it must take thousands of years, and the American Board estimates that 500,000,000 heathen go to hell every thirty years. Confining ourselves, however, simply to the Christian era, we have Dr. Skinner's authority for saying that, at the present date, there are 37,640,000,000 souls in the prison hell of which Dr. Hodge speaks, and they are all doomed to everlasting woe!

The prospect that the entire world will be converted to Orthodox Christianity seems at present very remote. So long as it preaches such doctrines as this, we cannot be sorry at the delay. " We hear much," said Dr. Channing, " of efforts to spread the gospel; but Christianity is gaining more by the removal of degrading errors, than it would by armies of missionaries who should carry with them a corrupted form of the religion." [1] Nevertheless, according to the common Orthodox view, every year of delay adds "twenty millions a year" to the number of heathen in hell! Rev. Gordon Hall, a missionary in 1812, supposed a hundred years — "a longer time," he said, "than is allowed by the ablest commentators" — would pass away before the introduction of the millennium. And then, in making an appeal to the churches, he added this significant question. "But what must become of the souls who are to appear on the earth *between this and the millennium?* To this momentous question Orthodoxy answers, *The vast majority are doomed to endless woe.*" And Dr. Barnes and Dr. Hodge add a tearful " Amen."

All the comfort, therefore, that can be extracted from this millennial hope, is the thought that God's government, and the scheme of redemption, is not such a practical failure as it seems to be, on the supposition that only a small fraction of the human family will enjoy its blessings. The harvest of saved souls, it assumes, is larger than the lost, and therefore the divine husbandry is vindicated. The vindication is only numerical. It is not moral. The

---

[1] " Moral Argument against Calvinism." Works (new edition), p. 408.

fact still remains, according to Orthodoxy, that millions —
yea, billions on billions — of lost souls have been consigned
to eternal damnation ; the fact still remains that there are
"twenty million souls" going to hell every year. God's
moral government cannot be vindicated by a system which
confines the blessings of salvation to a hypothetical multitude, in a remotely future era, while the vast majority of
those who have lived for nineteen centuries on the globe
are forever lost. This palliation is but another form of
the Calvinistic doctrine of election. God chooses the millennial age to display his glory, and saves the nations in
bulk; he reprobates all preceding ages, except the small
remnant of elected individuals that are saved from the
great mass. God becomes generous, merciful, and kind
in the millennial age ; but in all preceding ages he is un-
merciful and unkind, — a Shylock sticking to the bond,
clamoring for the covenanted pound of flesh, and willing
to take it not only from Antonio, — Adam, — but from all
his descendants.

Dr. William Rankin Duryee, although urging this millennial mitigation, is not without a natural suspicion of its
insufficiency. He says :[1] —

" If the men who cherish infidel or restorationist doctrine still
affirm that even such hopeful probabilities do not relieve the
subject of its sorrowful darkness, the believer throws the whole
matter on God, and will not exhaust his strength in vain ques-
tionings or vainer feelings. The Bible says there is some sin
from which is no redemption. As far as sentiment goes, one
soul eternally lost is as painful to contemplate as ten millions of
souls. And the sentiment, which sorrows over what God reveals
as His own will, is simply maudlin."

In his distrust and condemnation of the sentiments,
Dr. Duryee showed himself a Calvinist of the old-time
school. It has been the reproach of Calvinism that it
has dishonored the sentiments, especially the sentiments

[1] Christian Intelligencer, February, 1883.

of mercy and love, which are most outraged by this doctrine. And now with this horrible spectacle of millions of doomed souls before us, we are coolly told that "the sentiment, which sorrows over what God reveals as his own will, is simply maudlin!" This was the reproachful sentimentality that Jesus showed when he mourned over Jerusalem, and when he pathetically wept at the tomb of Lazarus. What maudlin sentiment that David should sorrow for Absalom; or that Paul, yearning over Israel, should be willing to be accursed for his brethren and kinsmen according to the flesh!

The remarkable confession of Dr. Barnes, which we print in the preceding chapter, furnishes one type of modern Calvinism, that which reveals the power, depth, and authority of the sentiments. Dr. Duryee's article shows another type, that which suppresses or ignores them. If the latter type has the impassivity of stoicism, the first has the virtue of being humane.

The ease with which Dr. Duryee quenches the sentiments, and disposes of the mistaken compassion to which the human heart is prone at spectacles of woe, is seen still further in the following passage : —

" All kinds of compassion are not the types of the Divine compassion. There is a sympathy with sin which may easily be mistaken for sympathy with sorrow. There is a sympathy with those whose punishment is deserved, which God and just men alike despise. When the Christian finds out at last who are in the regions of despair, and what they are there meeting, *we are very sure he will neither be affected by the number, nor by the duration of their punishment.*"

Those Christians who have not entirely lost the "maudlin" sentiments of mercy and love will not need any refutation of this passage. Believing, as they do, that the sympathy which arises from these sentiments is never despicable, and that a condemnation of sin is quite compatible with a sympathy for the sinner, they will be more concerned to ask what apology can be made for Dr. Duryee, for making in the year 1883 such extraordinary statements. Dr. Duryee would probably scorn any such service, and thus make the need of an apology only more apparent.

In defence of his position it may be said that the indifference of Christians in this life to the eternal woe of the heathen, when they have some power to prevent it, may furnish reason for the inference that Christians in heaven will be much more indifferent to such misery when they have no power to arrest it. But the indifference of Christians in this life is not a virtue. We agree with Dr. Skinner, Mr. Pond,[1] Bishop Colenso, and a host of other missionaries, that it is only a reproach if the doctrine be true. We take it as an evidence, however, that the doctrine is not true, since it is not possible for humanity to act as if it were true.

Another apology — not wholly sufficient, we grant — for Dr. Duryee's statement may be found in the fact that it is not new. Jonathan Edwards, Nathanael Emmons, Andrew Welwood, and others have presented its grateful and benumbing consolations to the saints with equal positiveness, and with more enthusiasm and power.

Dr. Emmons has told us that " We know that one part of the business of the blessed is to celebrate the doctrine of reprobation." [2]

Jonathan Edwards considered the subject of so much importance that he devoted an entire sermon to its development. The sermon bears this comforting title: " The End of the Wicked Contemplated by the Righteous; or, the Torments of the Wicked in Hell no Occasion of Grief to the Saints in Heaven." In this sermon Edwards first depicts the horrors of hell: —

[1] See his admission quoted in the previous chapter, p. 94.
[2] Works, vol. ii. p. 402.

" The miseries of the damned in hell will be inconceivably great. When they shall come to bear the wrath of the Almighty poured out upon them without mixture, and executed upon them without pity or restraint, or any mitigation; it will doubtless cause anguish and horror and amazement, vastly beyond all the sufferings and torments that ever any man endured in this world; yea, beyond all extent of our words or thoughts." (*Works*, vol. iv. p. 280, Worcester ed.)

Then he shows by contrast the joy of the saints in glory : —

" The saints in glory will see this and be far more sensible of it than now we can possibly be. They will be far more sensible how dreadful the wrath of God is, and will better understand how terrible the sufferings of the damned are; *yet this will be no occasion of grief to them. They will not be sorry for the damned ;* it will cause no uneasiness or dissatisfaction to them; but on the contrary, when they have this sight, it will excite them to joyful praises.

" The damned and their misery, their sufferings and the wrath of God poured out upon them, will be an occasion of joy to them. . . . " (p. 290.)

To make the application of the sermon more effective, Edwards paints a fearful picture of the separations that must take place at the last day : —

" How will you bear to see your parents, who in this life had so dear an affection for you, now without any love to you, approving the sentence of condemnation, when Christ shall with indignation bid you depart, wretched, cursed creatures into eternal burnings ? How will you bear to see and hear them praising the Judge, for his justice exercised in pronouncing this sentence, and hearing it with holy joy in their countenances, and shouting forth the praises and hallelujahs of God and Christ on that account?

" When they shall see what manifestations of amazement there will be in you at the hearing of this dreadful sentence, and that every syllable of it pierces you like a thunderbolt, and sinks you into the lowest depths of horror and despair ; when they shall behold you with a frighted, amazed countenance, trembling and astonished, and shall hear you groan and gnash your teeth ; these things will not move them at all to pity you, but you will see them with a holy joyfulness in their countenances, and with songs in their mouths. When they shall see you turned away and beginning to enter into the great furnace, and shall see how you shrink at it, and hear how you shriek and cry out ; yet they will not be at all grieved for you, but at the same time you will hear from them renewed praises and hallelujahs for the true and righteous judgments of God in so dealing with you." (p. 296.)

" As to those who are damned in hell, the saints in glory are not concerned for their welfare, and have no love nor pity towards them; and if you perish hereafter, it will be an occasion of joy to all the godly." (p. 297.)

In another discourse Edwards represents the happiness of the saints as greatly heightened by the contemplation of the eternal misery of the lost : —

"The sight of hell torments will exalt the happiness of the saints for ever. It will not only make them more sensible of the greatness and freeness of the grace of God in their happiness; but it will really make their happiness the greater, as it will make them more sensible of their own happiness; it will give them a more lively relish of it; it will make them prize it more. When they see others, who were of the same nature, and born under the same circumstances, plunged in such misery, and they so distinguished, O, it will make them sensible how happy they are. A sense of the opposite misery, in all cases, greatly increases the relish of any joy or pleasure." (*Sermon on the Eternity of Hell Torments.* Works, vol. iv. p. 276.)

In his rhapsodical book entitled, " Meditations representing a Glimpse of Glory: or, A Gospel-Discovery of Emmanuel's Land," [1] Andrew Welwood, a Scotch layman, vividly describes the joys of the saints in witnessing the tortures of the damned : —

[1] The date of the first edition we do not know. An American reprint was made in 1744; and editions were published in Pittsburg in 1824 and in London in 1839. It has undoubtedly been a very popular book.

" What joy! to behold Truth vindicated from all the horrid Aspersions of Hellish Monsters. I 'm overjoyed in hearing the everlasting Howlings of the Haters of the Almighty; what a pleasant Melody are they in mine Ears? O eternal *Hallelujahs* to JEHOVAH and the LAMB! O sweet! sweet! My Heart is satisfied. We committed our Cause to thee, that judgeth righteously; and behold, thou hast fully pleaded our Cause, and shalt make the Smoke of their Torment for ever and ever to ascend in our Sight." (p. 107, ed. 1744.)

Again the rapturous author says : —

" The beholding of the smoke of your torments is *a passing delectation.*" .(p. 109.)

That this doctrine which Welwood assisted to popularize in England is not wholly extinct there is shown by the testimony of Dr. Momerie, embodied in the following paragraph from the London *Inquirer* of March 10, 1883 : —

" We are sometimes told that the hideous doctrine of Eternal Torment is dying out, at least in its more repulsive aspects. The Rev. Dr. Momerie, Professor of Logic and Metaphysics in King's College, London, and one of the Select Preachers before the University of Cambridge, gives unimpeachable testimony that we are apt to overrate the progress of liberal sentiments in other churches. In his recent work on ' The Basis of Religion ' he says that only a year or two ago he heard a clergyman deliver himself from the pulpit as follows: ' My brethren, you may imagine that when you look down from heaven, and see your acquaintances and friends and relatives in hell, your happiness will be somewhat marred. But no! You will then be so purified and perfected that, as you gaze on that sea of suffering, it will only increase your joy.' For our part, we should prefer hell itself to a heaven where such hellish joy would be possible."

Unfortunately for the progress of liberal ideas we cannot affirm, as we should be happy to do, that this view of the indifference of the saints in heaven to the tortures of the damned in hell is obsolete in this country. Dr. Duryee has revived it anew, and presents it as a merciful mitigation of this doctrine of the doom of the majority. But it is a mitigation which does not mitigate. It does not relieve the damned, but only the elect. At the best it is a selfish view. The saints are fearful lest their happiness in heaven should be disturbed by the proximity of hell. "No," says Dr. Duryee, "when the Christian finds out at last who are in the regions of despair [parents or children, brothers or sisters, wives, mothers, or friends we have loved on earth], and what they are there meeting [tortures so horrible that no tongue can describe them, and so lasting that eternity cannot exhaust them], *we are very sure he will neither be affected by the number, nor by the duration of their punishment.*"

Whatever the effect of Dr. Duryee's attempted apology may be upon the school of Calvinists to which he belongs, we rejoice to believe that there are a vast number of Christians who still retain a sufficient amount of humanity to feel that this attempted mitigation only adds a new horror to those it seeks to relieve. It is the doctrine of annihilation applied to heaven instead of to hell—the annihilation of the sentiments of mercy and benevolence. The wicked are allowed to retain these sentiments in hell; Dives is represented as exercising them; but for the comfort of the saints they are extinguished in heaven. This view of heaven makes it, morally considered, several degrees lower than hell.

PROBATION AFTER DEATH.

Whatever comfort the doctrine of the annihilation of the sentiments may afford to ransomed or expectant saints, it does not relieve the character of God of the reproach of partiality and injustice. Dr. Schaff, after admitting the objections, adds:—

"The only solution seems to lie either in the Quaker doctrine of universal light—that is, an uncovenanted offer of

salvation to all men in this earthly life — or an extension of the
period of saving grace beyond death till the final judgment for
those (and for those only) who never had an opportunity in this
world to accept or reject the gospel salvation. But the former
view implies a depreciation of the visible Church, the ministry
of the gospel, and the sacraments. The latter would require a
liberal reconstruction of the traditional doctrine of the middle
state, such as no Orthodox church — in the absence of clear Scripture light on this mysterious subject, and in view of probable
abuse — would be willing to admit in its confessional teaching,
even if theological exegesis should be able to produce a better
agreement than now exists on certain disputed passages of the
New Testament and the doctrine of Hades." (*Creeds of
Christendom*, vol. i. p. 793.)

Of these solutions, that of probation after death is being
earnestly presented by the more liberal section of the
Orthodox body. The active discussion that has been held
has revealed the fact that there is a growing number who
find relief in the thought that those who do not have an
opportunity to receive the gospel here, may have it offered
to them hereafter. This view, if generally accepted,
would not relieve the subject of its darkest and worst
feature; but it would certainly lessen its horror. It
assumes that every one must have an opportunity to
receive the gospel before he can justly be punished for
rejecting it. It does not deny the dogma of endless
misery; but it refuses to confine to this life the probation which human souls are supposed to undergo. It
thus relieves the character of God of the charge of
damning the heathen and all others who die in ignorance
of the gospel. It throws some rays of divine mercy
across the grave. It is a reaction against the severity of
Calvinism. Arminianism has less need of this mitigation,
because it commits to the divine mercy and judgment
those whom the gospel has not reached. On the other
hand, this theory of probation after death is an improvement on the assumption held alike by Arminians and

Calvinists, that the destiny of the soul is fixed at death for all eternity.

The movement in favor of this doctrine is strongest in the Congregational body. Rev. Newman Smyth, D.D., of New Haven, and Professor Egbert Smyth of Andover, have been prominently before the public as its defenders. Mr. Joseph Cook, Professor Park, Dr. Goodwin, and many others have assailed it. The prolonged discussion it has received has helped to make the doctrine familiar and tolerable to many people; but it cannot be said to have received any general acceptance. The liberal element in the Congregational body is making a brave fight to estab-lish it. As a more merciful view of the divine govern-ment, its general adoption would be a grateful sign of progress. It is founded on noble conceptions of the divine justice and mercy. Once let such conceptions have full freedom, and the dogma of endless punishment will eventually be carried away like a rotten pier before a spring flood.

But while welcoming any extension of the sentiments of justice and mercy to theological discussions, we believe it is safest to found them on correct premises and to extend them on right lines. It is an essential defect of the move-ment in favor of probation after death, that it accepts most of the false premises on which Orthodoxy is built,— man's ruined nature, the necessity of an atonement, and the certainty of endless punishment for those who reject the gospel. We do not believe that any permanent relief can be obtained so long as these premises are admitted. Nor can we agree that this life, or any limited period in the next, is to be considered as a state of probation. Life is not a probation; it is a discipline, a school for character, a field for growth.

The only satisfaction, therefore, that we have in observ-ing the growth of the doctrine of probation after death, is in the hope kindled that it may lead to something better.

THE ESSENTIAL CHRIST.

Mr. Joseph Cook, having undertaken in his Monday Lectures to attack " Probation after Death," attempted to show that the Orthodox view of God's dealing with the heathen did not require this expedient. "God is immanent in the moral nature of every man," says Mr. Cook, "and whoever permanently accepts or rejects the innermost voice of conscience, accepts or rejects the essential Christ." This sounds very liberal and very plausible. It is precisely what Unitarians and other liberals have maintained for years. Paul stated it much better than Mr. Cook, without the possible confusion which may come from the term *essential Christ.* "God [who] will render to every man according to his deeds : . . . tribulation and anguish upon every soul of man that doeth evil, . . . but glory, honor, and peace to every man that worketh good." This is sound doctrine, and at the outset Mr. Cook seems to believe in it. To save his Orthodoxy, however, which would be practically destroyed by such an admission, he makes the following qualification : " Human nature is such, however, that only a *few among millions do accept the essential Christ of conscience.* A knowledge of the character, life, and death of the historic Christ must therefore be carried to the heathen and to the whole world." We do not wonder that the *Independent* was "startled" at this statement; we wonder that Mr. Cook was not startled by it himself. He has unwittingly drawn up an indictment, not against the heathen, but against the God who made them. If God has so constructed human nature that it cannot obey the laws of life he has prescribed for it, then the divine wisdom and goodness are at once impeached. In casting into the bottomless pit the clay which he has tried to form in his own image, the Divine Potter simply shows the failure of his own handiwork. Mr. Cook opens the door to the heathen, only to slam it in their faces when they try to enter. He practically records himself as one who believes in the damnation of the majority. The " fair chance " he offers to the heathen to get into heaven is considerably less than they would have of reaching the opposite shore in safety, if required individually to cross Niagara on a tight-rope.

VI.

UNMITIGATED FEATURES.

THE palliations we have considered are of interest mainly as showing the need that is felt among a large class for some relief from the distressing features of this doctrine. None of them, however, furnish a relief that is adequate. They have not yet been accepted by Orthodoxy. They are arguments for the revision of the historic creeds, but the desired revision has not been made. Merely to file off the rough edges of the old creeds will not suffice. The objections we urge are not merely against Orthodox standards, but against the Orthodox system which they represent. That system, as it is now held and taught, cannot be reconciled with the justice, goodness, and mercy of God. That it is no malice which prompts this statement may be seen from the Evangelical admissions, protests, and attempted mitigations which we have brought together in the two preceding chapters.

These objections are not simply metaphysical or logical ; they are above all things ethical. The ethical basis on which the old theology was constructed is one which has been outgrown. Civilization and society have advanced, but theology still clings to its mediæval God. Nothing but the voice of authority, urged as the voice of God himself, is able to support a theistic conception which would otherwise be promptly rejected as irrational and unjust. These ethical difficulties are not confined to this special dogma ; they belong to the whole theological system upon

8

which it is built. But they appear conspicuously in two or three aspects of this doctrine; namely, in the relation which God is supposed to hold to the number, the character, and the state of the doomed.

1. The Number of the Doomed.

Orthodoxy teaches that God "passes by" the far larger portion of the human race in conferring the blessings of salvation, and deliberately remands them to a fate from which his love and mercy might have saved them. We say "passes by," for that is the expression used in the Westminster Confession: "God was pleased, according to the unsearchable counsel of his own will, whereby he extendeth or withholdeth mercy as he pleaseth, for the glory of his sovereign power over his creatures, to *pass by* the rest of mankind, and *to ordain* them to dishonor and wrath for their sin, to the praise of his glorious justice." This "glorious [?] justice" operates to condemn to death the great majority of the heathen world, without even giving them a chance to accept the gospel which would save them. As one of the most prominent of Orthodox theologians, Dr. Philip Schaff, says, in a passage to which we have previously referred : —

"Everybody must admit that the vast majority of mankind, no worse by nature than the rest, and without personal guilt, are born, and grow up in heathen darkness, out of the reach of means of grace, and are thus, as far as we know, actually 'passed by' in this world. *No Orthodox system can logically reconcile this stubborn and awful fact with the universal love and impartial justice of God.*" (*Creeds of Christendom*, vol. i. p. 793.)

Dr. Channing, in considering this doctrine, that "the vastly greater portion of the human race is abandoned by God," was moved to earnest remonstrance : —

"It is the doctrine of the mass of Christians even now, that the heathen are the objects of God's wrath. All who live and die beyond the sound of the Gospel, it is thought, are doomed to endless perdition. On this ground indeed it is that most missionary enterprises rest. We are called upon to send the Gospel where it is not preached, because men conceive that, beyond the borders of Christendom, God is an implacable Judge; because no other parts of the earth are believed to hold communication with heaven; because it is feared that the human being, whose fate it is to be born a heathen, carries to the grave an inherited curse that will never be repealed. Well do I remember the shock once received from reading a missionary address, in which the speaker computed the thousands of the heathen world who would die during the few hours of the meeting; and he asked his hearers to listen in thought to their shrieks as they descended into hell. But how can a sane man credit, for an instant, that the vastly greater portion of the human race is abandoned by God? If Christianity did actually thus represent the character of God, we might well ask what right we have to hold or to diffuse such a religion. For among all the false gods of Heathenism, can one be found more unrighteous and more cruel than the Deity whom such a system offers as an object for our worship? But the Christian Religion nowhere teaches this horrible faith. And still more, no man in his heart does or can believe such an appalling doctrine. Utter it in words men may; but human nature forbids them to give it inward assent. Were the Christians who profess it deliberately to consider what such a doctrine means, and bring it home to themselves as a reality, — could they distinctly once conceive that every hour, by day and night, thousands of their fellow-beings are plunged by the never-ceasing anger of God into an abyss of endless woe, — how could they endure even to exist? They would look on this world as a hell, and long to escape from the sway of its merciless despot. No! The human heart is a far better teacher than these gloomy systems of theology. In its secret depth it believes, what perhaps it dares not to put into words, in God's Impartial, Equitable, Universal, and Parental Love." (*The Universal Father*, Sec. I. 4.)

In 1837 the New School Presbyterians of this country,

in the so-called Auburn Declaration, adopted the following article: —

"While repentance for sin and faith in Christ are indispensable to salvation, all who are saved are indebted, from first to last, to the grace and Spirit of God. And the reason that God does not save all is not that he wants the *power* to do it, but that in his wisdom he does not see *fit to exert that power further than he actually does*." (Schaff's *Creeds of Christendom*, vol. iii. p. 779.)

Channing has not stated more strongly, in an equal number of words, the moral difficulties of Orthodoxy, than they are stated by Dr. Schaff in the passage above, or than they are unconsciously revealed in the Auburn Declaration. How can we believe in the goodness and mercy and justice of God, and yet suppose that those who have had no opportunity to hear the gospel are to be banished to eternal night? God knows their condition; there is room enough in heaven for them all; he can save them if he will; it is not possible, says Orthodoxy, for them to be saved without him. Nevertheless God passes them by without mercy, and surrenders them to an endless misery to which he alone has ordained them.

The old Calvinistic doctrine of reprobation, in which Emmons and Edwards delighted, that God positively reprobated to death those whom he did not choose to save, is not held so sternly by modern Calvinists. They are content to say that God chooses some to salvation, and passes by or leaves the rest in the ruin in which the fall of Adam has plunged them, "not that he wants the power" to save them, "but that in his wisdom he does not see fit to exert that power further than he actually does." The trouble with this attempted alleviation is that it softens the *will* of God without softening his *heart.* The old Calvinistic God exerted his power; he cast souls into hell. The new God withholds his power, and they slide in by themselves. There is little choice between such descriptions of God. The immoral grandeur of the first can be as easily defended as the immoral languor of the second.

Is this the result of the teachings of Jesus Christ? Is this a fair representation of his view of the Father? There is a little story which Jesus himself told, which shows how he would have regarded this view of God:—

"A certain man was going down from Jerusalem to Jericho; and he fell among robbers, who stripped him and beat him, and departed, leaving him half dead.   And by chance a certain priest was going down that way; and when he saw him, he passed by on the other side.   And in like manner a Levite also, when he came to the place, and saw him, passed by on the other side.

" But a certain Samaritan, as he journeyed, came where he was ; and when he saw him he had compassion on him, and went to him and bound up his wounds, pouring on oil and wine; and he set him on his own beast, and brought him to an inn, and took care of him.   And the next day, as he was about to leave, he took money from his purse and gave it to the host, and said: Take care of him; and, if you spend any more, I will pay you when I come back.

"Which of these three, said Jesus, do you think was neighbor unto him that fell among the robbers?

" He that took pity on him.

" Then said Jesus, Go and do thou likewise."

Now the defect of the Orthodox theology is that, instead of deriving its ideal of God from the Good Samaritan, it has taken it from the Priest and the Levite. Humanity, it assumes, has fallen. It lies wounded and bleeding by the roadside. And yet the Almighty, the infinite Father, *passes by* on the other side. He sees his child groaning before his eyes; but, although it has fallen by the sin of another, he puts forth no hand to save it. What words could express human indignation at the conduct of such a Father? And if we knew that, by the cruel neglect of this unnatural parent, the wounded child was left to be torn to pieces by wild beasts, or that he was captured by savage tribes and subjected to months of slow torture and finally death, we should hold the father as a murderer, and remand him to the universal execration of mankind.

If such would be our feelings toward an earthly parent, how much more intensely should we repudiate all views of God which charge him with a neglect more culpable and a cruelty more intense. Let not this doctrine of the damnation of the heathen be charged upon Jesus Christ. The tenth of Luke and the fifth of Matthew are a lasting rebuke to the Westminster Creed and all who hold it. If we think of God at all, we must think of him not as being worse, but as infinitely better than humanity. So thought Jesus, and therefore urged men to be like unto him : —

" Ye have heard that it hath been said, Thou shalt love thy neighbor and hate thine enemy: but I say unto you, Love your enemies, bless them that curse you, do good to them that hate you, and pray for them which despitefully use you and persecute you, that ye may be the children of your Father which is in heaven; for he maketh his sun to rise on the evil and on the good, and sendeth rain on the just and on the unjust. Be ye therefore perfect, even as your Father which is in heaven is perfect."

2. The Character of the Doomed.

Another remarkable ethical defect of this doctrine is that it represents God as ignoring profound moral distinctions.

1. *God ignores moral distinctions in treating the innocent as if they were guilty.*

The astounding statement is made that by the sin of Adam the whole race partakes not only of the consequences of his sin, but also of his *guilt*. Adam was the representative of the race, says Calvinism; when he fell, the race fell with him. Every human being is born into the world steeped in original sin and under the penalty of eternal death. Even the innocent babe, dying without any consciousness of sin, without, in fact, consciousness of its own existence, cannot be saved without the application of the atoning blood of Christ to its soul; and according to the belief of Catholics and Lutherans we can only be sure that this blood has been applied when the child has been sprinkled with water.

We object to this view that it is merely a theological fiction, — that it is not true, and that it would be unjust if it were true. If men are born into the world with a nature so corrupt that they cannot obey the law of God, it is unjust to punish them for its violation.[1] Guilt can only follow where there is sin; sin is only possible to creatures that have moral ability. In punishing creatures that are only theoretically sinful, God would show himself to be only theoretically just. The assumption, however, that all men are born totally depraved we assume to be false to begin with. It is contradicted by the facts of human nature; it is contradicted by the example and precepts of Jesus Christ, who presented the humility and purity of childhood as an ideal to his own disciples by which they were to enter the kingdom of heaven.

Modern Calvinists and Arminians, believing that all dying in infancy are saved, attribute their salvation to the atonement of Jesus. But such a view is unjust to God. It supposes that God regards infants as guilty of sin. On the contrary we affirm that children are not guilty of sin until they are able to commit it, and that if not guilty of sin, they require no atonement for their salvation.

2. *But God also ignores profound moral distinctions in treating the guilty as if they were innocent.*

---

[1] Rev. Dr. D. D. Whedon, editor of the *Methodist Quarterly Review*, in his article on "Arminianism" in *Johnson's Cyclopædia*, forcibly states a moral and logical objection to Calvinism · "If a man is to be damned for fulfilling God's decrees, ought not that imaginary God to be *a fortiori* damned for making such a decree?" (Vol. i. p. 253)

A large and influential part of Protestantism has revolted against the assumption that men are only punished for the guilt of Adam. It is assumed therefore that all men *actually* transgress the infinite law, and are thus liable to an infinite penalty. The degree of the transgression is not important. All that is necessary is to commit an infinitesimal sin, to incur the judicial sentence of eternal torture. That all men sin we may readily admit; that any justly deserve infinite punishment for a finite sin we cannot grant for a moment. The object of this device is to defend the justice of God in bestowing punishment by assuming the guilt of the sinner. If, however, we grant, as we are asked to do, the actual as well as the inherited guilt of the sinner, we find that, although God may observe moral distinctions in damning men, yet he ignores moral distinctions in his method of saving them. The saved have no righteousness of their own. They are polluted and corrupt before God. Does the divine mercy save them? No. Orthodoxy will not allow it to operate here where its blessing is so much needed. It may operate in the *choice* of those who are saved, but not in the method of their salvation. How then are the guilty saved? Simply because God *agrees to consider them righteous on account of the righteousness of his Son.* They are not *actually* righteous; but righteousness is *imputed* to them.

It is not possible to transfer righteousness from one moral being to another. If a man incurs debt through immorality, it does not make him any better, any more righteous, if a friend pays the debt for him. We cannot put righteousness on or off as if it were a garment. Judas would still have been Judas, if he had worn the robe of Jesus. The only way righteousness can be achieved is in the way Jesus achieved it himself, through moral experience. God therefore ignores moral distinctions if he treats the guilty as if they were innocent.

3. *God ignores actual moral distinctions in choosing those who are saved.*

We say *actual* distinctions. We mean those distinctions which are recognized as real and positive in this life. We know that these distinctions are not taken as the basis for Orthodox theology. Its ethical theories are as original and hypothetical as its facts. The distinction it makes between a " righteous man " and a " sinner " is not the distinction which is made in the community; it is not the distinction which corresponds to character. We do not mean that Orthodoxy considers good character in this life unimportant; far from it; but it assumes that good character in this life has nothing to do with obtaining salvation in the next. Salvation is obtained only through the merits of Christ's blood. Only those are saved whom God has chosen to this privilege. If God chose only the good and the virtuous and the noble and the benevolent, we might infer that his choice was made with reference to some moral judgment. But according to Orthodoxy this is not the case. The most abandoned sinner is chosen as readily as the saint. Let the sinner but repent an hour before his death, and express belief in the atonement of Jesus, and he is saved. The man, however, who has lived an irreproachable life, who has endeavored to observe the Golden Rule and the two great commandments, who has tried to obey his own conscience, to do justly, to love mercy, and to walk humbly with God, — such a man, if he does not accept the Orthodox " plan of salvation," is hopelessly lost.

Mr. Spurgeon, in his commentary on Psalm ix. 17, " The wicked shall be turned into hell, and all the nations that forget God," thus expresses his conviction in regard to the good character of the damned.

" How solemn is the seventeenth verse, especially in its warning to forgetters of God. The moral who are not devout, the honest who are not prayerful, the benevolent who are not believing, the amiable who are not converted, — these must all have their portion with the openly wicked in the hell which is prepared for the devil and his angels. There are whole nations of such. The forgetters of God are far more numerous than the profane or profligate; and, according to the very forceful expression of the Hebrew, the nethermost hell will be the place into which all of them shall be hurled headlong." (*Treasury of David.*)

Is it not clear then that God ignores actual moral distinctions, when he allows " the moral," " the honest," " the benevolent," and "the amiable," to go to the " nethermost hell " ?

But a small proportion of the good people of the world are gathered into the Christian Church; and if it be true that only those who " accept Christ" are saved, there will be but a small proportion of the good in heaven. Some of the grandest souls that have ennobled human life and character have been reared under the name and influence of paganism. Though they have not professed the Christian religion, they have " been diligent to frame their lives according to the light of nature and the law of that religion they do profess; " yet, if the Westminster Catechism, and the system of theology which it represents, be true, they cannot be saved in any way whatsoever, and " to assert and maintain that they may is very pernicious and to be detested."

One of the charges brought in 1874 against Rev. David Swing of Chicago, on his trial for heresy, was that he had used language contrary to this section of the Confession of Faith : —

" He [David Swing] has used language in respect to Penelope and Socrates which is unwarrantable and contrary to the teachings of the Confession of Faith, Chap. X. Sec. IV. ; that is to say, in his sermon entitled ' Soul Culture' the following passage occurs: ' There is no doubt the notorious Catherine II. held more truth and better truth than was known to all classic Greece — held to a belief in a Saviour, of whose glory that gifted land knew nought; and yet such is the grandeur of soul above mind, that I doubt not that Queen Penelope, of the dark land, and the doubting Socrates have found at heaven's gate a sweeter welcome, sung of angels, than greeted the ear of Russia's brilliant but false-lived queen.'" (*Specification* 12.)

No matter what the purity and moral altitude of a heathen soul may be, "the heathen in mass," according to Dr. A. A. Hodge of Princeton, "with no single definite and unquestionable exception on record, are evidently strangers to God, and going to death in an unsaved condition." [1]

Precisely the same rules which exclude Penelope, Socrates, Epictetus, Plato, Plutarch, Confucius, and Gautama, exclude also Channing, Emerson, Parker, Garrison, Lincoln, Longfellow, Spinoza, Humboldt, Darwin, and a numerous host of "the moral," "the honest," "the benevolent," and "the amiable," from the joys of the future life. It is therefore clear, according to Orthodoxy, that God not only chooses *but a few* from the whole race to be saved, but that he ignores all actual moral distinctions in selecting this number, and therefore but a small percentage of the good can reach heaven.

The moral enormity of this doctrine is thus clearly exhibited in the inevitable conclusion to which it leads, that not only the great majority of the race, *but the great majority of the good*, are doomed to endless woe.

3. The State of the Doomed.

It is not merely the number and the character of the majority that make this doctrine hideous, but it is the nature and extent of the doom they suffer — *a misery indescribable in its severity and unending in its duration.*

It is a sufficient condemnation of the Orthodox view of God that, in dooming the great majority of the race, his practical and moral government of the universe is proved

[1] Com. on Conf. of Faith, p. 242.

to be a failure. It is a still greater condemnation of the system that God is represented as ignoring all practical moral distinctions in choosing the saved, while he violates the principles of justice and mercy in condemning the lost; but the climax of injustice is not reached until we remember the utter horror and endlessness of the misery to which they are consigned.

We have directed this treatise against a point in regard to which Orthodoxy seems to have developed an unexpected sensitiveness. Certain modern Calvinists are indignant that Orthodoxy should be represented as teaching that the *majority* are doomed, while they manifest no indignation whatever at the nature and extent of the doom which this majority must suffer. Yet it is the severity and endlessness of the punishment which makes the number of its victims of importance.

Dr. William Rankin Duryee has said that "so far as sentiment goes, one soul eternally lost is as painful to contemplate as ten million souls."[1] It depends somewhat upon the nature of the sentiment invoked. The sentiment of justice has a problem to deal with in considering why God should create the greater part of the human race simply to damn them for his glory, which it does not have in considering the damnation of a single unrepentant soul; but to the sentiment of pity we do not know which seems more pathetic, to contemplate billions of human souls in endless torment, or to think of a single lost soul left in utter loneliness in the eternal abyss. Perhaps, if we had the ingenuity of Emmons, we might discover a flickering indication of divine benevolence in the very fact that God, out of pity to the few, damns the vast majority, that they may enjoy together that company which misery is said to love. "Solitude," says Donne, "is a torment which is not threatened in hell itself."[2]

---

[1] Christian Intelligencer, Feb. 14, 1883.

[2] Works, vol. iii. p 513.

Certainly not, if we accept the official estimates of the American Board as to the number of souls hell contains — estimates based on accepted data of Orthodox theology. One of the Schoolmen, quoted by Donne, declared, however, that hell could not be possibly above three thousand miles in compass, and that one of the torments of that place would be its crowded state.[1] And it is apparent that neither Emmons nor Edwards, nor any modern exponent of the horrors of that place, intends that we shall derive any comfort from the fact of numbers.

It is evident, therefore, Dr. Duryee being our witness, that no mere alteration in the number of the lost can remove the darkness of the destiny to which the lost are consigned. Upon this point Calvinism and Arminianism stand on the same plane. Arminianism has nobly protested against the doom of the majority, but it has failed to protest against the doom of the minority. It has sought to make God less cruel and vindictive, it has endeavored to throw the responsibility of future punishment upon man instead of God, it has recoiled with indignation from the doctrine of reprobation, it has refused to believe in the condemnation of the heathen in mass, it has offered the atonement to all; but, with individual exceptions, Arminianism has taught, and still teaches, the *endless misery* of all those who fail, during a probation confined to this life, to accept the gospel. Methodism has been the resolute opponent of Universalism; it has vied with Calvinism in depicting, with lurid and painful particularity, the fearful and unending state of those who fall into hell. If it were the purpose of this treatise to show what Evangelical denominations have taught concerning the horrors of hell, we should hardly know whether Arminian or Calvinistic annals furnished the more abundant material. The prominence which this doctrine has had in both systems, and the frequency with which its terrors have been

[1] Works, vol. iii. p. 325.

exposed, render any further delineation of its physical and mental horrors unnecessary. It has been the especial task of those who have believed in an endless hell to exhibit, for greater effect, the agonies it imposes on its victims. The books, sermons, and tracts which have been printed to illustrate it would fill a good-sized library; and we may thank heaven that by far the larger part of the myriads of sermons preached to propagate it have escaped the printing-press and suffered a just oblivion. A brief reference to the titles collected by Dr. Abbot, in his Bibliography of the Future Life already referred to, will show how many treatises have been devoted to the special work of depicting endless horrors. Jonathan Edwards is more widely known to-day for his famous descriptions of hell-torment than for other things which deserve better to be remembered. The resources of human ingenuity and of human language seem to have been exhausted in inventing forms of torture through which the divine wrath may be exhibited during the unending cycles of eternity.

At the present day delineations of the physical terrors of hell are less common. Only the uneducated perhaps would maintain with Charles Wesley that —

> " A real, fiery, sulphurous hell
>   Shall prey upon our outward frame; "
>
> (*Hymns on God's Everlasting Love*, Hymn XI. p. 23.)

But the Orthodox conviction of the severity of the torture has been in no degree relaxed. Its form has been changed only to add to its intensity; and those who no longer believe in a physical fire still assert with Wesley : —

> " But sorer pangs the soul shall feel
>   Tormented in a fiercer flame."

It matters little whether we are taught that the damned are forever burned in a lake of fire and brimstone, whether they are remanded to the tortures of a Satanic persecutor, who shares with God the glory of their pain; or whether they are simply abandoned to the more excruciating tortures of. a sleepless conscience, or affections lacerated by eternal separation from all that is lovable. In any case the suffering is represented as the most extreme that the human mind can conceive, while its duration is described as absolutely unending.

If, as we have said, it has been the especial task of believers in an endless hell to expose the physical and mental horrors of the doctrine they have taught, it has been reserved for those who oppose the doctrine to point out its *moral* enormities. If the pictures drawn of the state of the damned are horrible, the picture of God presented is still more horrible. We cannot avoid the conviction that the damned are morally superior to a God who, with malignant hate or cruel indifference, would consign them to a fate which they have in no measure deserved. All attempts to found this doctrine upon rational premises utterly fail. It is in its very nature irrational and arbitrary; and it can only exist under the supposition that God is a tyrant to be feared, and not a Father to be loved and obeyed.

The conception of law is totally opposed to a punishment which is lawless in its execution; and all ethical considerations are violated when we find God meting out infinite punishment for a finite sin. Of all the lame apologies which Orthodoxy has been driven to make in its behalf, none avail to remove the fearful moral difficulties of this doctrine, and the terrible reproach it casts upon the character of God.

That retribution for acts done in this life may extend to the next, and that the vast majority of mankind may have much to repent of, we do not deny. Such a conception is rational and ethical; but it is the fearful curse of *endless* woe that makes future punishment hideous. It assumes that evil must forever continue in the universe, and that Infinite Goodness has no power to subdue it; or if God's power be acknowledged, it assumes that he is not willing to exert it, and thus while his power abides, his goodness perishes.

The doctrine of endless punishment, and the idea of God that accompanies it, belongs to an age that is past — an age of superstition and cruelty. It is a belief which could never yield the fruits of righteousness and peace. It does not draw men toward God; it drives them from him. Its practical results have been such as we might ' expect from so cruel a theory. Rev. Stopford Brooke justly claims that "the doctrine of eternal punishment ought to be denied because of its evil fruits."

" A good tree does not bring forth corrupt fruit, and we owe to this doctrine all the slaughter and cruelty done by alternately triumphant sects in the name of God. It gave birth to the Inquisition ; it drove the Jews to unutterable misery ; it burnt thousands of innocent men and women for witchcraft ; it tortured and rent the bodies and souls of men ; it depopulated fertile lands ; it ruined nations ; it kept the world for centuries in darkness, held back civilization, and in all ages urged on the dogs of cruelty and fanaticism to their accursed hunting." (*Eternal Punishment:* a sermon, preached at Bedford Chapel, London, Nov. 5, 1882.)

None too severe is this bold arraignment. If this doctrine has not always been the direct and immediate cause of such cruelties, it has sprung from the very spirit that created them, and has powerfully assisted in their perpetuation. Men have appealed to the cruelty of God to justify the cruelties which they have wrought with their own hands. And what are the practical effects of the doctrine to-day? Mr. Brooke has observed them in England and thus speaks : —

" Those were its fruits in the past, and on this account we .ought to deny its truth. But now we ought to fight against its lies day by day; for we who do not believe it have no notion of the harm it is doing to those who do believe it. We are bound to contend against it if we have any desire that a nobler Christianity should prevail among men, for its teaching drives men into infidelity and atheism. The less educated classes—who yet feel strongly, and more strongly than the educated, the things of the conscience and the heart—say that it denies all their moral instincts. And so it does. It makes them look on God as an unreasoning and capricious tyrant, and they turn from him with dread and hate. It makes them consider the story of redemption as either a weak effort on the part of an incapable God to save man, or as mockery by him of his creatures, on the plea of a love which they see as derisive, and a justice which they see as favoritism. And till we free the teachings of Christianity from this doctrine, religious teachers will still continue to give, as they do now, the greatest impulse to infidelity among the working-classes, an impulse much greater than any given by all the materialism of philosophers or all the mouthing of iconoclasts." (*Ib.*)

There are grateful signs that this doctrine is losing its hold upon the popular mind. The Evangelical churches find it less politic to use it as an aggressive weapon. Formerly the doctrine was used to defend the authority of the Church; at present the Church is obliged to defend the authority of the doctrine. It still stands in all its grimness on the church creeds, but apologies are required for its presence there. One of them lies before us. It is a tract entitled "Eternal Destruction," issued by the Presbyterian Board of Publication, Philadelphia, in 1882, to show "that eternal death, or everlasting destruction, is both *reasonable* and necessary, as the highest penalty under the divine government." "Our object," says the author, "is rather to tone up the faith and correct the errors of many who, while professing to hold fast to the doctrine of future punishment as set forth in the creeds of the Evangelical churches, do it, nevertheless, with apparent misgivings, and when they speak of it are wont to say in substance that it is a terrible mystery that such a doctrine is contained in a revelation from the God of

9

infinite love, and that they could not receive it were it
not for the positive teaching of inspiration. If they attempt to use the terrors of future retribution as a part of
God's message to sinful men, they do it so *delicately*, and
with such softening circumlocution, as fairly to suggest
that either the Evangelical ministry of the present day do
not half believe the doctrine of endless punishment, or
that they have not the courage to preach it. And those
who repeat this saying care perhaps very little which of
these alternatives is true, for the want of courage to declare one's convictions must imply that such opinions are
passing out of the general belief of the community."

That such a defence should be necessary shows the
higher ethical demand which compels it. That the Presbyterian Board should be willing to make it, shows, on the
other hand, the tenacity with which this doctrine is clung
to as an essential part of the Orthodox system. It is a
belief which is destined to die, but not without a long
struggle. It behooves those who have once held it, to
make a continued and earnest effort to relieve other minds
of the darkness which it casts over the horizon of life.
There is no surer way of contributing to its extinction,
than by insisting that ethics shall have the authority in
theology that it has in common life. Theology has practically ignored the profoundest moral relations. It cannot regain its authority until it bows to the moral law
that it has ignored.

VII.

THE SOLUTION.

It would be a painful task to expose the "dark and
awful" features of the doom of the majority, if we did
not know that there is a brighter and nobler view of God
and human destiny which should displace it. It is un-

doubtedly true, as we have said before, that the great mass
who hold this doctrine, only nominally believe it. It does
not affect their happiness, because they never realize its
fearful import. Human nature has other resources besides
logic with which to protect itself against superstition. As
a bullet may be encysted in the body, so a painful and unnatural belief may become encysted in the mind. Yet there
are thousands of devout, earnest, and thoughtful people
who are periodically sensible of the oppressive weight of
this dogma. They would gladly be relieved of the burden if they could but see how it might be rolled off. To
such minds Orthodoxy offers no help. The logical superstructure of Orthodoxy has been carefully built. So long
as the foundation premises are acknowledged, its conclusions inevitably follow. The whole system is based on an
ancient but palpably false conception of the universe. The
false premises must be removed before we can expect to
destroy the false conclusions.

In denying the premises of Orthodoxy we do not, necessarily, deny those of Christianity. The fundamental
principles of all religions are far deeper than the theological systems that are built upon them. Indeed, it is
by a re-assertion of essentially Christian principles that
we find a corrective for many of the errors that have
been taught in Christianity's name. Infant damnation,
for instance, is historically a dogma of Christian theology;
yet nothing could be more diametrically opposed to the
original principles of the Christian religion. If the gos-
pels be not a lie, Jesus treated little children as if they
were the offspring of God, not as if they were the offspring of the devil.

What, then, is the natural, rational, and ethical relief
for this doctrine of the doom of the majority? It is not
one of our own invention. If it were simply a private
and personal solution we should hesitate to offer it; but
it is one towards which the spirit of the age is irresistibly

moving. We are merely reporting its utterances. It is a solution which is an outgrowth of broader and healthier conceptions of God and humanity, and a more enlightened view of the functions of reason, ethics, and religion. We have not space to unfold it at length; we can only briefly indicate some directions in which its influence is evident.

1. A More Enlightened View of the Bible.

The doctrine we have endeavored to refute is not a congenial one to the reason or the heart. It would promptly be abandoned by the majority who hold it, if it were not supposed to rest on Biblical authority. The creeds which contain it are authoritative mainly because they are presumed to be a correct exposition of the Bible on the points they cover. Hence, in the endeavor to refute the Orthodox view of this doctrine, much attention has been necessarily directed towards a better interpretation of the Scriptures. The discussion has long been waged on the battle-ground of exegesis. This has not been without valuable and helpful results. Unfortunately, however, it has usually been conducted under the limitations imposed by an erroneous view of the Bible itself. It has been assumed that there is no appeal from its acknowledged teaching; that it concludes all debate on the subjects of which it speaks; that it is divinely inspired and infallible. Bound by this view of the infallibility and dominant authority of this collection of books, the only resource which has been left to those who accept it, when struggling against doubtful or uncongenial teachings, has been to exercise a desperate ingenuity in the interpretation of texts. The temptation has been strong on one side to admit only traditional interpretations, or those which harmonized with an accepted theological system; on the other side, the temptation has been to make the Bible mean always what we would like to have it mean. The integrity of the intellect has been sacrificed to quiet the moral

sense or to allay disturbed emotions. Much has been read
into the book that does not belong there, and much has
been read out of it that it really teaches. This has been
occasioned wholly by the unjust claims made in its behalf,
and the artifices to which men have resorted in evading
them.

In an address which excited wide attention, and which
led to the debate on the special topic of this book, Rev.
George E. Ellis, D.D.,[1] said with great truth : —

" *Orthodoxy cannot readjust its creed till it readjusts its estimate
of the Scriptures.* The only relief which one who professes the
Orthodox creed can find, is either by forcing his ingenuity into
the proof-texts or indulging his liberty outside of them. All the
most vital and searching forces now at work in their bearing
upon themes of loftiest import to man demand, and are working
toward, the intelligent and fearless reconsideration of the accepted view of the Bible, which opens the most teasing contro-
versies, which deals with them all in a most unsatisfactory way,
and leaves them all unsettled, if not more perplexed.

" Here is a volume of miscellaneous and heterogeneous contents, some of them written we know not when, where, or by
whom, all of which are unified as from one divine source and
authority. In that volume is matter, instruction, warning,
precept, and promise of priceless and transcendent value for the
life and the hope of man. For that, it is consecrated and
bedewed with the most sacred of human affections. Because
of such contents, that book has become to Christendom a
gracious gift of God. We refer to its influence, with that of
the steady progress of material and physical science which it
has helped to quicken and guide, — all the most elevating, refin-
ing, beneficent, and regenerating agencies which are advancing
and redeeming humanity.

" Now look at that book from the other side, as what is called
Church History centres around it. There are matters in that book

---

[1] " The Position of the Liberal Body as affected by the Rupture
in the Orthodox Body of Congregationalists," *Christian Register*, Nov.
16, 1882. See also additional statements of Dr. Ellis in issues of the
same paper for Nov. 23, 1882 ; Jan. 18, 1883.

which, if they have not been the cause, have been the occasion, the agency, the instrumentality, backed by an assumed divine warrant, of strifes, feuds, superstitions, persecutions, barbarities, and atrocities of every stain and hue, which have strewn the world for ages with wrecks of woe and agony. I will not fill up that outline. I shudder over the summary; and I cannot challenge the charge which assigns all this to the estimate and use of the less lovely, the less benedictive lessons of the Bible. President Mather of our young college, for many years the most eminent and honored man, citizen, and divine in this colony, expressly taught that the divine command to the Israelites to exterminate the Canaanites was a full warrant for the desolation of our Indian tribes. Search to the bottom the history of that delirium of dread and frenzy and outrage which we call the witchcraft delusion here, nearly two centuries ago. You will find but a single palliation for the agency of good and upright men in those horrors. Judges, witnesses, yes, even the victims, read in a book — which they had all been taught to believe, and did believe, was written by the finger of God — this sentence: ' Thou shalt not suffer a witch to live.'

" It is not alleged by any one that there is a single sentence in that book which was written with intent to deceive or mislead. But there is much in it, with the authority and purpose claimed for it, which has grievously misled many of the best of our race, and which does so now. A steadily increasing number of persons of all grades and classes in intelligence, sincerity, and devoutness, leave that book from year to year through a long life unopened. Not as preachers complacently say, because of their sin-hardened hearts, for very many of them are seeking and longing for some blessed religious guidance. It is because what they remember and hear said about the book, as coming direct from God, perplexes, astounds, and shocks them. There are those who continue to be readers, and who share those feelings, publishing their doubts and denials, often with ridicule and scorn. They find in the book commands, purposes, and acts assigned to God, at which they would shudder if ascribed to heathen deities. Standing on this modern earth and beneath these ancient heavens, men boldly, sometimes sadly, say that there are assertions and statements in that book which they know positively to be untrue, — untrue to fact, to history, to the verities

of nature and life, to the attributes and rule of the Being to
whom their loftiest and most devout convictions rise as the God
over all. A clerical discussion upon the point whether Scripture
texts can be interpreted so as to allow a hope for idiots, infants,
and heathen, who have had an 'imperfect probation' here,
does not reach to their relief. When a few of those texts are
alleged as certifying that the vast majority of the human race
are to be the victims of endless woe, the questions cannot be
silenced: 'Who wrote those words, and with what authority?
Were they correctly reported and duly certified?'"

In these words Dr. Ellis goes to the very bottom of the
difficulty. A scholarly, conscientious exegesis may furnish
some relief; but no adequate and satisfactory solution is
possible until the Orthodox estimate of the inspiration and
infallibility of the Bible is revised. Justice to those who
wrote these books, as well as to those who read them,
requires such a revision. A candid study of the book
shows, we believe, that the Orthodox view of the Bible is
not taught in the Bible itself. Like the doctrine of the
Trinity, it is something imposed upon it.

Before we can test anything by the Bible, we must test
the Bible itself. The tests we may employ are threefold
— historical, rational, and ethical.

THE HISTORICAL TEST.

Whence, when, and how, we must ask, did this collection
of books come? Who wrote them, whom did they address,
and to what end? How was this collection put together,
under what influences, and by whose decision?

The simple historical answer, which we cannot present
in detail, shows that the Bible grew up precisely as other
sacred books grew, — that, while it records miraculous
events, it has no miraculous history itself. It was written
in Hebrew and Greek, by different men of widely different
character, during an interval of a thousand years. The
original manuscripts have not been preserved. The copies

that exist vary sufficiently to make an infallible text impossible. No truthful man can put a copy of the Greek or of the Hebrew Testament into the hands of a reader of these languages, and say, "Here is the book just as it was originally written." There are many manuscripts to choose from, and the best Hebrew and Greek text of the Bible is that which shows the best human judgment and the widest and most accurate scholarship in its selection.

Still further, historical research shows that the books which compose the Bible were not bound together by the command or indication of God; they were selected by men. We have no evidence that the judgment of Christian communities, leaders, or councils was infallible. On the contrary, the Christian Church has never agreed as to the number and selection of books which constitute the Bible. Thus, Augustine had one Bible, and Jerome another; the Roman Church has one Bible, and the Protestant another; the Swedenborgians one Bible, and the Orthodox another. The history of the formation of the Bible Canon is a refutation of the claim that is made for the infallibility of the book. "It is clear," says Dr. Samuel Davidson,[1] "that the earliest Church Fathers did not use the books of the New Testament as sacred documents clothed with divine authority, but followed for the most part, at least till the middle of the second century, apostolic tradition orally transmitted. They were not solicitous about a Canon circumscribed within certain limits." And in regard to the principle which guided selection Dr. Davidson says: —

"The exact principles that guided the formation of a Canon in the earliest centuries cannot be discovered. Definite grounds for the reception or rejection of books were ·not very clearly apprehended. The choice was determined by various circumstances, of which apostolic origin was the chief, though this

[1] Article on "The Canon," in *Encyclopædia Britannica*, ninth ed., vol. v. pp. 9, 10.

itself was insufficiently attested; for, if it be asked whether all the New Testament writings proceeded from the authors whose names they bear, criticism cannot reply in the affirmative. . . .

" Instead of attributing the formation of the Canon to the Church, it would be more correct to say that the important stage in it was due to three teachers, each working separately and in his own way, who were intent upon the creation of a Christian society which did not appear in the apostolic age, — a visible organization united in faith, — where the discordant opinions of apostolic and sub-apostolic times should be finally merged. The Canon was not the work of the Christian Church, so much as of the men who were striving to form that Church, and could not get beyond the mould received by primitive Christian literature."

Luther exercised the right of private judgment very freely in regard to the books which should compose the Bible. Esther, he thought, did not properly belong to it. The Apocalypse he "considered neither apostolic nor prophetic, but put it almost on the same level with the Fourth Book of Esdras, which he spoke elsewhere of tossing into the Elbe." [1] The Epistle of James he thought an "epistle of straw;" and he denied apostolic authorship to James, Jude, and Hebrews. If Luther could be so free and independent in judging the authority of whole books, why may we not judge with equal freedom the authority of special texts?

If God had seen fit to make an infallible book, we may be certain that he would have surely indicated what books or chapters should belong to it, and that he would not have left its interpretation such a doubtful matter. The Roman Catholic Church has consistently maintained that an infallible interpretation is necessary to an infallible revelation.

It is evident therefore, on external and historic grounds, that there is not the slightest foundation on which to build this dogma of Protestantism.

---

[1] *Ibid.*, p. 14.

THE RATIONAL TEST.

If there is no external authority for the interpretation of the Bible, we must judge it by its contents. We must apply to it precisely the same tests that we apply to all other books. If the Bible appeals to reason, we must judge it by the laws of reason. If the Bible contradicts reason, reason may justly contradict the Bible.

Bishop Butler clearly recognized the rational test: —

"I express myself with caution, lest I should be mistaken to vilify reason; which is indeed the only faculty we have wherewith to judge concerning anything, even revelation itself; or be misunderstood to assert, that a supposed revelation cannot be proved false from internal characters. For it may contain clear immoralities or contradictions; and either of these would prove it false." (Butler's *Analogy*, Part II. ch. iii. p. 219, Bohn's Ed.)

Again : —

"Reason can, and it ought to judge, not only of the meaning, but also of the morality and the evidence of revelation." (*Ib.* p. 229.)

Dr. Channing did noble service in maintaining the office of reason in testing and interpreting the Bible. "How," he asked, "is the right of interpretation, the real meaning of Scriptures, to be ascertained? I answer, By Reason. I know of no process by which the true sense of the New Testament is to pass from the page into my mind without the use of my rational faculties. In truth, no book can be written so simply as to need no exercise of reason." In another passage, Dr. Channing says: —

"If I could not be Christian without ceasing to be rational, I should not hesitate as to my choice. I feel myself bound to sacrifice to Christianity property, reputation, and life ; but I ought not to sacrifice to any religion that reason which lifts me above the brute and constitutes me a man. I can conceive no sacrilege greater than to prostrate or renounce the highest faculty which we have derived from God. In so doing, we should offer violence to the divinity within us." (*Christianity a Rational Religion.*)

Again, in the same paper, he said: "We must never forget that our rational nature is the greatest gift of God. For this, we owe him our chief gratitude. It is a greater *gift than any outward aid or benefaction*, and no doctrine which degrades it can come from its Author."

On this ground, which Channing took, we may maintain a firm stand. The Bible is a noble gift from humanity to humanity; but reason is still nobler and diviner, because it is the witness we have that we are the offspring of the Eternal Mind.

It is clear that reason must use to-day all the light that eighteen centuries of increased knowledge may throw upon the topics which the Bible treats. We need no longer turn to Genesis to learn the story of the creation of the world or the origin of man, or to explain the diversity of human speech. Modern science can read the story of creation more correctly from a still older Genesis. Historical questions are to be determined by untrammeled historical criticism, and all questions involving rational judgment are to be decided on rational principles, or by appeals to human experience.

Some years ago the writer attended a prolonged debate in Utah, between Orson Pratt and Rev. Dr. J. P. Newman, on the subject, " Does the Bible sanction Polygamy?" The Mormon marshalled texts with considerable skill, and the debate concluded with a hot battle over the interpretation of a certain text in Leviticus, which began with a " Thus saith the Lord," the one side contending that it prohibited polygamy, and the other that it permitted it; and the Hebrew language suffered evident violence in the endeavor to make it mean one thing or the other. It was a striking proof of the futility of appealing to an infallible book without an infallible interpretation. As rational method would have transferred the discussion to another field, and decided it not by a text in Leviticus, but by the common sense, the moral judgments, and the experience of humanity.

THE ETHICAL AND RELIGIOUS TEST.

If reason is necessary to test the truth or error of any given part of the Bible, the ethical and religious test is still more necessary. *We must decline to accept as authoritative any interpretation of the Bible, be it true or false, which affronts the moral sense of humanity or impugns the righteousness of God.*

The savage barbarities of the early Hebrews, for instance, in the slaughter of their enemies, are defended because done by divine command. We apply the ethical test, and are forced to decide that God could not and did not command any such atrocities. They are sufficiently explained by the existence and unrighteous manifestation of human passions, and find sad parallels even in our own day. We cannot suppose that God ever literally commanded a Hebrew father to sacrifice his child upon an altar, even if merely to try his faith. The story of Abraham is an illustration of the ruling idea of early ages; and we see how the patriarch, in climbing the mountain, reached also higher and truer ideas of God. The moral standard of the early Hebrews was lower than that we accept to-day, and therefore is not to be received as authoritative, unless confirmed or corrected by later and higher tests.

It is from a failure to apply the ethical test to the Bible, that Orthodoxy has reared upon it a theological system which, as Channing well said, " owes its perpetuity to the influence of fear in palsying the moral nature." "Its errors are peculiarly mournful, because they relate to the character of God. It darkens and stains his pure nature, spoils his character of its sacredness, loveliness, glory, and thus quenches the central light of the universe, makes existence a curse, and the extinction of it a consummation devoutly to be wished." [1]

---

[1] Moral Argument against Calvinism.

The moral darkness of that system is sufficiently illustrated and abundantly acknowledged in the evidence we
have presented in relation to this doctrine. In justice to
the Bible, it may be necessary critically to study its pages
to see if it teaches it; but, when we are asked to decide
about the *truth* of the doctrine itself, exegesis has nothing
to do with it. The dogma must be tried at the bar of
reason and conscience; and, when these condemn it,
its doom is sealed. The Bible is not the test of Ethics,
but Ethics must be the test of the Bible. Says Dr.
Channing : —

"Reason must prescribe the tests or standards to which a
professed communication from God should be referred; and,
among these, none are more important than the moral law which
belongs to the very essence and is the deepest conviction of the
rational nature." (*Christianity a Rational Religion.*)

"How dangerous it is to read the Scriptures without carrying
into their interpretation our reason and the light of conscience!
. . . The free, bold language of the Apostle has been perverted
from its original significance, and made to support a system
which reason and conscience revolt from, and which transforms
Christianity from the gospel of glad tidings into the saddest
message ever preached." (*The Universal Father.*)

IS THE BIBLE AN ORTHODOX BOOK?

Not until we have put aside, as unbiblical, unreasonable,
and untenable, the Orthodox view of the nature and
origin of the Bible, and are prepared to treat it simply as a
collection of religious and historical books of purely human
origin, resting on the same basis with all other religious
books, are we in a position to ask what the Bible is, and
what it teaches. Only then can we approach it without
theological bias. We shall then find that it does not teach
the system of Orthodoxy, or any exact system of theology.
The doctrinal unity of the book is utterly broken. It was
written at different times, by different men, under the

influence of different ideas. It shows growth, development, diversity. A monotheistic conception dominates both of its divisions; but there is just as much difference between Jahveh, the jealous God of the early Hebrews, and the tender, loving Father whom Jesus worshipped, as there is between the God of Calvin and the God of Channing. The Canticles have no more reference to Jesus than have Virgil's Eclogues. The writer of the fifty-third chapter of Isaiah no more thought of Jesus, when he wrote that chapter, than he thought of Abraham Lincoln; and the lesson of the chapter is as applicable to one as to the other, illustrating a grand truth which the whole history of the world plainly reveals, that " without shedding of blood there is no remission." Only through the blood of its martyrs has humanity been lifted to a higher plane of truth. Difference, diversity, opposition, and development are seen in the New Testament. Paul did not teach the miraculous birth of Jesus; the Synoptics do not give the speculations of Paul; while the Gospel of John, written under Grecian influence, presents a different view of Jesus from the more Hebraic one of the Synoptics.

Though it would be unjust to Orthodoxy to say that none of its doctrines can be supported by Biblical texts, and that some of them are not natural growths on Biblical soil, yet we believe that the Bible, taken *without the constraint of this theory of infallibility*, and interpreted on the same principles on which we should determine the meaning of a Greek or Latin classical author, does not yield the Orthodox system.

There is another branch of study which greatly helps in deciding this question, and that is the department of Church History. When we interrogate it, we find that Orthodoxy, as a system, has not sprung full-formed from the Bible, but that it is of much later origin and growth. An effectual refutation of many of its errors is found

when we trace them back to their inception, and note the
influences that have shaped them, and the false premises
on which they are based. The doctrines of the Trinity,
the deity of Jesus, total depravity, the atonement, endless
punishment, the infallibility of the Bible, — in short, the
very doctrines which Orthodoxy still regards as essential,
— are all subjects of post-Biblical growth and development. In regard to the doctrine of the Trinity, for instance, supposed by Orthodoxy to be fundamental, there
is not one passage in the Bible, from Genesis to Revelation, which can be imagined to be a statement of it; which
even *sounds* like saying "in the unity of the Godhead
there are three persons, the same in substance, equal in
power and glory." Not only is there no clear passage in
which any writer of the New Testament, speaking in his
own name, has called Jesus Christ *God*, in any sense, but
on the contrary, he is everywhere as clearly distinguished
from the "One God, the Father," as a distinct person or
being, in the ordinary sense of the words *person* or
being, as Peter is from John. He is everywhere represented, not as "equal in power and glory" to God, but as
subordinate to him and dependent upon him. If Jesus
Christ were to return to the earth to-day we believe he
would be profoundly surprised at the Christianity which
has been and still is taught in his name. His own disciples misunderstood him ; and humanity has repeated,
perpetuated, and multiplied their mistakes. The Bible
has been a quarry to which men could go and, whenever they needed, find a text as the corner-stone for some
doctrinal theory. The stones thus wrenched from the
original strata have been shaped and fashioned in church-
councils, synods, presbyteries, and in the brains of profes-
sional theologians. From age to age the design of the
edifice has been changed, and redecorated and elaborated.
John Calvin was the master architect who rebuilt the
system, and secured for it his name. When we compare

the Calvinistic system with the Christian one, they differ as much as a mediæval cathedral differs from the boundless sky under whose well-beloved benediction Jesus delighted to preach. Calvinism can only accommodate a few; Christianity is large enough for all.

Whatever appeals may be made to the strong Oriental imagery of special texts of the New Testament, in which the idea of retribution is figured, the number of Christians is increasing who refuse to believe that he who preached the beatitudes, and told the parables of the Good Samaritan, the Prodigal Son, and the Ninety and Nine, ever meant to teach either the damnation of the majority or the endless misery of a single human soul.

The assumption of the infallibility of the Bible, and the kindred assumption of the infallibility of the Pope, both arose from the endeavor to preserve the authority of the Church. One assumption is as insupportable as the other, and we do not know which is the more mischievous. Humanity will have nothing to lose, but everything to gain, from abandoning them.

The Bible has been the test of Truth; now Truth must be the test of the Bible. All that is just, pure, and true in that book, all that helps and comforts, all that is inspired because it inspires, will be gratefully preserved. Its errors, or the errors which have been built upon it, will be gently and firmly laid aside. As Dr. Ellis has truly said: "That the sanctities of that book may be retained, the assumptions and superstitions associated with it must be surrendered." [1]

The removal of false notions concerning the absolute authority of the Bible will lead to a more sympathetic attitude toward the sacred literature of other peoples, and the religions which they represent. The damnation of the heathen has been frequently defended on account of their idolatry. Even such a serious writer as Dr. Shedd, in his

[1] Christian Register, Nov. 16, 1882.

sermon on "The Guilt of the Pagan," presents this as one charge in the indictment. Yet the conception of God which the heathen often entertain is morally superior to that of the God who is preached to them in the name of Christianity. The idolatry of the heathen, instead of establishing their guilt, is their vindication. It is but another proof of the presence and aspiration of the religious sentiment. The heathen who bows down to wood and stone is more evidently human, more evidently religious, than if he bowed to nothing.

This more sympathetic attitude towards other religions, instead of diminishing our consciousness of the divine light which shines upon the pages of the Hebrew-Christian Bible, will help us to a recognition of the breadth, fulness, and perpetuity of the divine manifestation. There is an older and a larger Bible, whose Genesis was "in the beginning" and whose Revelation has not closed. Not only unto us, but unto all the nations, hath the Divine Word spoken. God hath never left himself without witness, either in the works of nature or in the heart of man.

We have quoted from Channing to show that this rational and ethical test of the Bible was defended by his illustrious pen. We cannot better close this chapter than by reaffirming in his own words, from that admirable essay on "God Revealed in the Universe and in Humanity," our conviction that the revelation of God is not confined to the Christian Bible, but that it is as large as humanity, as boundless as the universe: —

"Divine Wisdom is not shut up in any one book. . . . We cannot find language to express the worth of the illumination thus given through Jesus Christ. But we shall err greatly if we imagine that his gospel is the only light, that every ray comes to us from a single book, that no splendors issue from God's works and providence, that we have no teacher in religion but the few pages bound up in our Bible. Jesus Christ came, not

10

only to give us his peculiar teaching, but to introduce us to the imperishable lessons which God forever furnishes in our own and all human experience, and in the laws and movements of the universe.

2. A Different Estimate of Human Nature.

Remove the stumbling-block of Biblical infallibility, and theology will sooner or later adjust itself to the facts of science and the demands of ethics. A more modern view of the nature and origin of man will follow. If the Bible be the architectural plan, the supposed fall of Adam is the corner-stone on which the Orthodox system rests. Take that away, and the logical superstructure falls. The order for its removal has already been passed, and is gradually being executed. This Semitic legend of the introduction of sin into the world has exercised an immense influence upon Christian theology. Its influence has been exerted, not in what it teaches so much as in what men have taught from it, — namely, that by this sin our first parents "fell from their original righteousness and communion with God, and so became dead in sin, and wholly defiled in all the faculties and parts of soul and body; they being the root of all mankind, the guilt of this sin was imputed, and the same death in sin and corrupted nature conveyed to all their posterity descending from them by ordinary generation. From this original corruption, whereby we are utterly indisposed, disabled, and made opposite to all good, and wholly inclined to all evil, do proceed all actual transgressions." [1]

The additions which have been made to the original legend may be seen by comparing this version of the Westminster Confession with the version in Genesis.

It is this sin of Adam which calls down the wrath of God, opens the pit of an endless hell, and requires an infinite atonement.

[1] Westminster Confession, VI. ii.-iv.

When, however, we learn that the story is simply a *legend*, and not the record of a fact, the poetry remains, but the horrible consequences disappear. Viewed through the light of science, and the revelations of history and philosophy, human nature is seen to be not ruined, but incomplete. Humanity has not hopelessly fallen; it has ascended by slow and toilsome climbing the lofty spiral of history. It has suffered checks and, in different branches, retrogression; but age by age its progress has been upward and onward toward the attainment of ideals which God has not failed to reveal to it. No curse of God flows in the blood of humanity, for " in him we live and move and have our being," " for we also are his offspring."

This rational view of the origin of human nature and its education and development lights up the whole track of history, displays the method of God in the education of the race, and, instead of hanging a dark pall over the unknown future, paints the prospect before us in cheerful colors of hope and trust.

There is a divine element in human nature, revealing to us our kinship with the Eternal. There are instincts, aspirations, and affections in the soul, which prophesy growth and development. It may be through the discipline of pain, through unremitting struggle; but it shall climb on the trellis which God has raised for it, and bear fruit in future ages on a higher plane. Our faith in the destiny of humanity is planted deeply in our confidence in God.

3. *A Nobler View of God.*

Our thought of God should ever be the product of our highest and best ideals. Under Calvinism this is not possible. God is surrounded by clouds and darkness; his moral glory is eclipsed. A more just conception of the character of God and his relation to humanity will require

a complete revision of the traditional theology. We cannot be satisfied with any representation of God which
makes him less just, true, and good than humanity. As
Dr. Ellis[1] truly says: "There cannot be two kinds of
justice, for God and man, any more than there can be
two kinds of mathematics, for measuring the fields of the
earth and the spaces of the sky." Our thought of God at
best is incomplete and imperfect. It is bounded by the
limitations of our nature. It must be to a great degree
anthropomorphic. The frames in which we picture God
as ruler, governor, creator, judge, cannot bound his in-
finitude. A larger and more grateful conception is that
of the Divine Fatherhood or Motherhood. It is meta-
phoric, limited, incomplete, as any image of human relations must be when reflected upon the truth, beauty, and
goodness of the Eternal Perfection; but it expresses more
fully than political or judicial metaphors the nature of
our relations to God. We are born of the life of God;
nurtured and sustained by his care, educated by his laws,
corrected by his discipline, guided by his providence, and
redeemed by his love. It was under the image of the
fatherhood of God that Jesus conveyed his most touching
lessons of the divine attitude toward humanity. How
beautifully that love is pictured in the parable of the
Prodigal Son! The father is not vindictive, cruel, or un-
forgiving; but when the son "was yet a great way off,
his father saw him, and had compassion, and ran and fell
on his neck and kissed him." If historical Christianity
may be charged with presenting conceptions of God that
are unworthy to be perpetuated, we must also gratefully
remember that it has likewise bequeathed to us tender
parables of the divine mercy and goodness, which shall
forever abide as proofs of the "light of the knowledge
of the glory of God in the face of Jesus Christ." The
parables of the Prodigal Son and the Ninety and Nine

[1] Christian Register, Nov. 16, 1882.

are far better pictures of the divine relations to the wayward and the "lost" than any of the cold, hard, creedal
statements of Evangelical theology. So long as he sins,
the Prodigal suffers; but when, in penitence and self-abne-
gation, he determines to return to his father's house, he is
received with open arms, and the fatted calf is killed for
the feast. No sacrificial offering, no *atonement*, in the
ordinary theological sense, is required of the son to pro-
pitiate the father. The wayward boy has suffered the
penalty of the laws he has violated. The father's joy is
that the son has henceforth determined to obey them.

This simple parable of Jesus exposes what we believe
to be a cardinal error in the Orthodox system, — namely,
the presumed necessity of a belief in the atonement of
Jesus as a condition of salvation. Some of the moral
objections to this view we have already pointed out. It
abrogates the divine law instead of honoring it. It teaches
that the actual consequences of sin may be averted by a
simple belief in the merits of the blood of Jesus. It
confers a righteousness which is imputative, not real. It
presumes that God needs to be reconciled to the sinner, as
well as the sinner to God.

The difficulties which the common view of the atonement presents disappear under a higher, broader, and
more rational conception of divine and human nature.
Human nature is not at enmity with God, and God is not
at enmity with human nature. God is present in humanity
and in the world, "reconciling the world to himself." The
natural and the spiritual world are not in conflict. The
laws of nature are manifestations of the life of God.
The will of God is not capricious or arbitrary; it is simply
the divine righteousness fulfilling itself. There is no
divine law, conceived in its universal aspects, but has some
element of good in it. The salvation of humanity is found
in reconciliation to the eternal truth, beauty, and goodness, — in the adjustment of the human will to that which

is divine. The end of salvation is not release from an arbitrary and unending punishment, but the attainment of perfection in character. No higher ideal has ever been raised for humanity than the ideal of Jesus: "Be ye perfect, even as your Father in heaven is perfect."

TRIUMPH OF THE GOOD.

Whatever figure we may choose in which to picture the divine character, none can be satisfactory to-day which does not represent God as absolute righteousness. It is our trust in the righteousness of God, joined to an equal trust in his infinite goodness and infinite power, which justifies and even compels our faith in the final triumph of the good. Evil is but a relative term; it cannot be a permanent element in the universe.

Our trust in God's goodness does not extinguish the idea of retribution in the next life; it may even require us to believe in it; since retribution is but a fulfilment of the divine law, and a part of the process by which humanity is purified and redeemed. Reason and faith alike forbid us to suppose that the sphere of human education, and the rewards and punishments which belong to it, is confined to this life. God is not hampered by time-limits in the development of a human soul.

"We cannot argue,"[1] says Channing, "that a being is not destined for a good, because he does not instantly attain it. We begin as children, and are yet created for maturity. So we begin life imperfect in our intellectual and moral powers, and yet are destined to wisdom and virtue. We are to read God's End in our inherent tendencies, not in our first attainments." If God is able in the ages to come to redeem humanity from the power of sin, faith in his infinite mercy and goodness requires us to believe that he will do it. Calvinists have tried to prove

---

[1] Trust in the Living God.

the glory of God in the damnation of the vast majority of the race; but how much more glorious do his justice and goodness appear in their redemption. If Edwards be true, there is joy in heaven over those that are lost; if Jesus be true, the joy in heaven is over those that are saved. The Divine Shepherd cannot allow a single one of his flock to perish. The lambs he carries in his bosom, and every one of his sheep he knoweth by name. There are ninety and nine in the fold; they have all been gathered in but one; yet the tender compassion of the Good Shepherd yearns with infinite pity over the sheep that is lost. It is the Good Shepherd himself who goes forth to seek it. No shade of the forest, no depth of the valley, no cavernous darkness, can conceal the lost and wandering one from the Shepherd's eye. The lost is found, and, gently folded in the Shepherd's arms, is brought to the fold. So a lost and wayward soul cannot wander in any part of the universe, cannot reach any depth of sin, where the love of God cannot find and save it. Not until every soul of the innumerable flock shall have been gathered into the divine fold will he see of the travail of his soul and be satisfied.

www.ingramcontent.com/pod-product-compliance
Lightning Source LLC
Chambersburg PA
CBHW021118020726
47500CB00003B/814